Quarry's BLOOD

by Max Allan Collins

A HARD CASE CRIME NOVEL

A HARD CASE CRIME BOOK
(HCC-151)
First Hard Case Crime edition: February 2022

Published by

Titan Books
A division of Titan Publishing Group Ltd
144 Southwark Street
London SE1 0UP

in collaboration with Winterfall LLC

Print edition ISBN 978-1-78909-668-2
E-book ISBN 978-1-78909-669-9

Design direction by Max Phillips
www.maxphillips.net

Typeset by Swordsmith Productions

The name "Hard Case Crime" and the Hard Case Crime logo are trademarks of Winterfall LLC. Hard Case Crime books are selected and edited by Charles Ardai.

Printed in the United States of America

Visit us on the web at www.HardCaseCrime.com

In memory of
JOHN LUTZ
and
PARNELL HALL,
two writers who were
as good as their words.

*"It seemed so illogical to punish
some poor criminal for doing something
that civilization taught him how to do...."*
CHESTER HIMES

*"Yet who would have thought the old man
to have had so much blood in him?"*
WILLIAM SHAKESPEARE

*"Showing or suggesting
an explicit awareness of itself;
self-referential."*
DEFINITION OF *meta*

1983

ONE

The Biloxi Strip hadn't cleaned up its act at all in ten years. I'd been here in chilly early spring that time too, which meant the *other* strip—the white-sand one between shimmering Gulf of Mexico blue and four-lane blacktop—was mostly tourist free now, barely a bikini in sight. But on the north side of Highway 90, titty bars, cheap motels, tattoo salons, and massage parlors proliferated like mushrooms, the kind you can't trust.

What had been Mr. Woody's was emblazoned now with neon script across the face of a former warehouse:

LOLITA'S
GENTLEMAN CLUB

The neon letters were switched on 24/7, but what you saw by day were the painted white letters behind buzzing pink electric ones. Two glass-brick windows in a facade of alternating vertical stripes of pink and black had on their either side angled announcements in red on a field of white:

TOPLESS DANCERS!
BOTTOMLESS DRINKS!

Backing into a place, almost up to a wire-mesh fence, I parked the chocolate-brown 1973 LeSabre, which I'd bought for a grand-and-a-half cash at a low-end used car lot near the airport. I strolled from lazy sunshine shy of warmth into a cold smoky artificial night where "Crazy Little Thing Called Love" was booming. A bouncer at the door—a big black guy in a black shirt and a gold dollar-sign necklace, his eyes hooded but not sleepy—told me there was no cover. That meant the drinks would be steep.

Nothing had changed much—the small round tables still were black, the padded faux-leather chairs red, a main stage erupted from the facing wall, a secondary stage (just a pole and a little platform) lurked at left. At right was the expected full bar with a female bartender in tuxedo shirt and string tie and tons of red permed hair; a few waitresses in the same uniform but with black minis and mesh stockings circulated flirtatiously. The late afternoon crowd had begun to pick up, the place half full, if you were an optimist, which you were if you thought the girl giving you a table dance was having fun, too.

The clientele divided itself in thirds—enlisted men, junior execs, and college boys, always in groups of at least three. A decade back, I'd have fit into either the first or third categories. Now—in my sportcoat and pastel shirt and skinny (but not too skinny) tie—I probably looked more like I belonged to the middle bunch.

The place seemed vaguely spruced up but not remodeled in any significant way. I hadn't changed radically either. I was 31, five ten, 170 pounds, my brown hair longer than the GIs and middle managers, yet shorter than the frat boys. Handsome enough to get laid occasionally but no stranger to a strip joint.

I drifted through the fog of smoke like a tramp steamer and docked at the underpopulated bar. The Coke with lime I ordered cost five bucks, which was no surprise; the Annie-afro bartender had a fetching smile and really seemed to dig me. Or maybe it was my keep-the-change ten-spot.

The girls on stage had worked bottomless ten years ago. Whether their g-strings meant the city was cracking down, so to speak, or rather reflected the current management's sense of decorum, I couldn't say. If I had to bet, it would be on the latter, as the owner was a former pole dancer who might have come to consider gynecological exhibitions demeaning. The latter may seem unlikely, but not as unlikely as the city of Biloxi growing a conscience.

The dancer on stage—a very pretty Asian girl with pert, real boobs and cascading brown hair—was strutting around to "Slow Ride," a garden of green growing out of her g-string; she would harvest it when her set was up. College boys sat ringside with their mouths open, baby birds wanting to be fed. The girl on the secondary stage was voluptuous if rather plain, though her overdone makeup strove mightily to overcome that. She had admirers, too. Boob men are a dedicated lot.

I'd been in town two days and inside this club four times. I had spotted the manager—the Lolita of the marquee—only one time per visit. Petite and looking younger than her twenty-eight years or so, she'd been a blonde and was now brunette; she wore pantsuits here, which played down her curves. Even so, it remained obvious the proprietress could have, had she felt like it, still worked the main stage.

She'd emerge from the door marked PRIVATE to talk to what- ever bartender was on duty briefly before disappearing behind that door again. Another black harem-style guard was posted there, arms folded with beer-keg biceps.

Even after four visits, she hadn't noticed me. Each time, I'd seated myself in back, at a small table, in sunglasses, which cut the glare of the red and blue revolving lights in the ceiling. I'd spent a good deal of time outside, as well—in the LeSabre in the parking lot, working surveillance. No, I'm not a cop.

When she'd come out for a chat with the bartender on my pre- vious four visits, no time pattern had revealed itself. Early after- noon once, late afternoon twice, mid-evening once. Tucking away my sunglasses, I was just figuring I'd have to ask the bartender to send my name back to the manager—who, a decade ago, had known me as John Quarry—when the PRIVATE door opened and Luann came out, wearing a purple pantsuit.

She saw me at once.

And froze.

For a moment, her lovely baby-doll features were as blank as a honeydew, if a honeydew had big blue eyes that could widen twice their size. Then she smiled, before going blank again. Apparently her latest trip for a word with the bartender could wait, because she immediately nodded at me—despite all the time that had passed since our last meeting—and curled her finger, summoning me like a child to a spanking.

She pushed open the PRIVATE door and paused, her back to me, waiting while I caught up. The harem guard eyed me suspiciously as I followed her through, but Luann didn't even glance back as I tagged after her down the cream-color cement-block hall. Behind us, somewhat muffled, "I Love Rock and Roll" began just as the next pair of strippers passed pleasantly by in a cloud of perfume that didn't quite disguise a secondary aroma of weed. At the end of the hall was a door marked MANAGER, where Luann went in and I followed.

The office hadn't changed much either, which was a surprise. Framed posters of famous strippers who'd appeared here in the Mr. Woody's era (Carol Doda, Candy Barr, Fanne Foxe) still crowded the modest space, looming over a metal desk, a few file cabinets, black-leather visitor chairs, and a matching couch, as well as a small fridge. No liquor cart now—she'd never been a drinker, something we had in common.

The last time Luann and I had been in this office, I had killed the previous manager as well as his wife. That is another story, but they were monsters so don't shed a tear. That information is pertinent only because it explains why my normally unflappable self was pretty fucking flapped.

It's also noteworthy that the only change Luann seemed to have made since we were both in this office last was to clean the blood off the furniture and walls.

The little doll of a woman, her complexion pale as milk, her pantsuit purple as grape juice, pointed to the couch and I obediently sat. She shut the door, locked it, came over, and sat on my lap.

She put her arms around me and kissed me, as if I were a serviceman returning from Vietnam to a loving wife's warm welcome. This was ironic in my case, since when I'd returned from Vietnam, my warm welcome had been to find my wife in bed with a guy, which led to my killing him a day later, but never mind. Anyway, I held up my end of the kiss, though it didn't go anywhere because we both had too many questions.

Her first one, after sliding off my lap into a sideways position on the couch, was: "What are you doing here, Johnny? I didn't expect ever to see you again!"

"You don't seem to mind," I said, smiling as I wiped lipstick off my mouth with a wrist.

"You don't either," she said, with a nod toward my tented trousers.

I said, mildly reproving, "I thought I told you to keep a low profile for a few months, then book it the hell out of Biloxi."

She nodded. "That was the plan. But I got the opportunity to buy this place cheap. And with all that money I had, why not? Anyway, Johnny, back then strip clubs was the only business I knew."

Which implied she knew more than that now.

I said, "You do seem to be doing all right."

Another nod. "None of my girls hook. No drugs allowed, not using or selling or anything. Well, grass, backstage, but that's all. On stage, my girls keep their pants on. Bet you noticed that."

"I don't know that I'd call those 'pants.' "

"They're called g-strings."

Luann had never had much of a sense of humor.

I fluffed some of the dark brown hair riding her shoulders. "And here I thought you were a natural blonde."

"No. I just use to dye it. Pussy hair, too."

"Guess I never noticed the roots of your evil."

She frowned. "I did my roots all the time."

See what I mean? Not that I'd managed much of a joke.

"Well," I said, "I have to say you do make a mean brunette."

"I'm not—"

"I know," I said, lifting a palm, "you're not mean. It's an expression indicating you make a good-looking brunette."

"I never heard that expression."

"You can make it through life without it. But to me, you'll always be a blonde."

She waggled a finger. "If you come back to hang around, Johnny, don't look for me to get a dye job for you. That caused too much trouble when I took this place over!"

"Why's that, Luann?"

She smirked in disgust. "Customers would hit on me all the time. Particularly if they knew me from before. They would ask me when was I gonna get up on that fuckin' stage and do my thing. But that's not my thing anymore."

"Well," I said with a shrug, "you're as beautiful as ever. And, hey, the club is named 'Lolita's,' and that *is* the name you danced under."

She made a face. "That's just a name. It's an old movie about an old guy who screws a teenager. I thought you *knew* movies. Anyway, just because a place is called McDonald's doesn't mean Old McDonald is flipping burgers in back."

I just looked at her. She had a gift for merging smart and

dumb in a fashion second to none. And, Christ—that last had been damn near a joke! I felt a warmth about her. She had turned up in my memories more often than most. She was the kind of girl you remember in the shower.

The muffled sound of "Hit Me With Your Best Shot" filtered in.

I asked, "Anyone helping you run this place? Any partners?"

"No. It's all me."

Those light blue eyes looked fantastic with the dark eye-shadow and all; when she turned those orbs loose on me, I felt like she was seeing through me, not in the figurative sense, but the literal.

She folded her arms. "I got my GED, Johnny. I took night classes and got an Associate Degree in business. I'm not stupid anymore."

Really she never had been. But her drug addict mother had sold her to the man whose office this had once been. Luann had been twelve.

"There's a difference between ignorant and stupid," I said, "and you were always smart, honey. And now you aren't even ignorant."

She smiled. It was a lovely thing. Perfect little teeth white as a toothpaste ad. I could damn near fuck her on this couch right here in this office where she witnessed me killing two people. But even after ten years, I couldn't quite get past the surroundings—on the wall, Carol Doda was looking at me with a sexy smirk. And this visit was, at the root of its evil, business.

Luann sensed that.

"Johnny, what are you doing here?" She was frowning, but in thought, nothing negative. "Are you still a hitman?"

The girl had always watched a lot of TV. That phony world was where she'd escaped when she was first pressed into whoring.

"No, I quit after about five years," I told her. I gave it to her matter-of-fact and she took it the same way. "I was kind of fucked in the head after Vietnam."

She nodded sagely. "Things you did there. Sniper, you said. And your wife screwing that guy. I remember. So you aren't doing that anymore? Killing people? For money?"

I winced. "Not exactly."

Frowning in thought again, she asked innocently, "How does somebody not *exactly* kill people?"

She was not stupid, as I hope you now can see, and she had acquired some education. But I still needed to keep it simple. Too much detail would just overwhelm her. And me.

From the club came a muffled "Thriller."

"There was a man called the Broker," I said, skipping *Once upon a time*, "who gave me assignments."

The frown was confused now. "School assignments?"

"No. Like—jobs for me to do."

She nodded slowly, the once-blonde hair bouncing on her purple shoulders. "Oooh. What *people* to kill. Got you."

I gestured casually. "He betrayed me and I had to handle it."

"You killed *him*." She was still nodding.

I gulped in air and let it out slow. She was buying what I told her, but somehow *I* wasn't—and, shit, I'd lived it!

I said, "I got hold of this sort of list the Broker had of other people like me…other 'hitmen.' I thought of a way I could help the people who these hitmen were hired to kill. I had the addresses…"

"Of the victims?"

"No. Of the contract killers. For a while now, I've been using the list to select hitmen to follow to their assigned targets…the persons they're hired to kill…and then I quietly approach those targets and offer my services."

She closed one eye and stared at me with the other; closing the eye pulled her mouth up on the same side. It was like she'd stopped mid-wink. "You tell them somebody's been hired to kill them, and then offer to stop it?"

She was skeptical, but had grasped the concept right away.

I shrugged, threw open my hands. "Yeah. That's pretty much exactly it."

"How do you do it?" she asked. Both eyes were open now, but the skepticism hadn't faded completely.

"Well, there's usually two people assigned to each job. One does surveillance." She would know that word from TV. "The other, working from information the surveillance guy provides, comes in and does the job."

"The hit."

"Yeah. It's called passive and active—one gathers intel..." She would know that, too. A lot of TV, this girl. "...the other executes the, uh, execution."

God.

She studied me. I wasn't sure whether she thought maybe I was lying to her, or possibly putting her on. Or that I'd gone insane. But, interestingly enough, the one thing I didn't sense in her was any fear.

And the skepticism seemed gone.

Finally she said, very quietly, hands folded in her purple lap, "You're doing this to make up for what you did before. To settle up. Redeem yourself, like they say in church."

I touched her folded hands, gently. "No, honey. I do it for money. The intended victims pay me to get rid of the hitmen and then find out who hired it. *Try* to find out, anyway. That last is the tricky part."

The blue eyes peered at me out of slits and this nod was barely perceptible. "You have to be a kind of detective."

"That's right." I shrugged a shoulder. "I haven't always succeeded. But usually? I do."

"When you find who hired the killing, you kill them?"

"That's it."

Luann just nodded, accepting all of it at face value.

"So," she said, as she sat sideways on the couch, "why are
you here? Not to look at the girls shake their booty or get a
great big kiss from me."

"No. I was glad to get that kiss, Luann...but no. I'm here
because I *followed* somebody here."

Not fear exactly, not even alarm, but the eyes got very big. In
surprise. This she hadn't seen coming.

She said softly, "A hitman."

"Yes."

"Followed a hitman *here*. To me."

"Yes. To you. To this place. And to that nice house of yours.
The passive guy has been on stakeout, watching you." She'd
know "stakeout" from TV, too.

Luann was nodding again. It was as if she'd been told her
business needed fumigating or her roof needed re-tiling.

"Well," she said, "I need your help, don't I?"

"You do."

I stood.

She looked up at me with those big light-blue eyes, though
they weren't alarmed or frightened. They trusted me. *What
next, Daddy?*

I held my hand out to her and said, "I need to show you
something. In the parking lot."

She took it, nodded dutifully, and rose.

She led me out into the corridor and back into the club, where
"You Shook Me All Night Long" was echoing. Outside, the
song became distant. Dusk's gentle blue had settled itself onto

the world. Four college guys went in, laughing, jostling.

I guided her to the LeSabre, backed up against a fence, no car parked on either side. About a dozen vehicles were in the lot but no other Lolita's patrons were out here, not at the moment anyway.

I walked her around behind the Buick, with only a foot or so between the fence and the trunk. I used the key and the lid rose to reveal two bodies, stuffed in there like clothes in a laundry bag. They didn't seem like people, just askew limbs and split-open heads, and the edges of the clear plastic tarp under them rose around them like the petals of a ghastly blossoming flower. They smelled bad, coppery blood and piss and excrement.

She regarded them unflinchingly; she did not even say "Ooow" or "yuck."

What she said was, "How did you get them both in there?"

I shrugged. "Took some doing. I had to put the spare in the back seat. That was the easy part."

"Putting the spare in the back?"

I shook my head as I shut the trunk lid. "Killing those two pricks."

I elaborated as we stood there in the darkening blue, the smell floating mercifully away on an ocean breeze. "I had to do it one at a time, at different places, over several days...but it's done. And I'll dump this car tonight on some back road."

"That's a good idea."

"But like I said...that's the easy part. Figuring out who sent them is where it gets difficult."

She shrugged, shook her head, the breeze taking the brown locks gently. "Not really."

"No?"

"I *know* who sent them."

We went back inside where the strippers who'd passed us in the hall were working the two stages to "What I Like About You." In her office, we discussed the details, including that I didn't expect her to pay me for my services but would appreciate having my expenses covered.

"I can do better than that," she said.

TWO

The Biloxi HQ of the Dixie Mafia hadn't changed much, either. Several blocks from Lolita's, the pale pink brick tower still announced itself in pink neon—

T
R
O
P
I
C
A
L

M
O
T
E
L

—next to the winking green neon outline of a palm tree. A tower among dinky, dingy neighbors, the Tropical had a corner double lot all to itself on the four-lane blacktop beyond which Gulf waters glimmered with the ivory of a nearly full moon.

The parking lot, as befitting off-season, was nearly empty. The windows onto the motel restaurant, the Dockside, betrayed only a handful of diners in booths. I parked the LeSabre, which still contained its trunk of two corpses and no spare. I had come straight from Luann's. Under my sportcoat was something I hadn't taken with me into her strip club: my nine-millimeter Browning automatic in a custom shoulder holster that allowed the weapon to ride with a noise-suppressor that doubled the length of its barrel. The jacket had been specially tailored for me as well. I was the shit.

Or was I just *a* shit? I was flying by the seat of my pants, improvising perhaps out of affection for Luann.

I went into the lemon-and-lime pastel lobby with its wicker furniture and potted palms and ambled to the front desk, where an attractive young blonde in a jacket that matched the lobby and lipstick that matched the jacket, smiled and asked me if I was checking in.

"Not just yet," I said. "I need to talk to Mr. Brunner. Alex Brunner? I believe he's in the penthouse."

She stiffened just a little, the smile turning brittle. "Are you on the list, sir?"

"Depends on the list. We're doing business. I'm from Atlanta, just got in. Do you have any vacancies, by the way?"

Judging by the parking lot, they had nothing but vacancies.

"We do, sir. But as for Mr. Brunner, if you could give me your name…?"

"I'll check in after my meeting, but for now, do you have any stationery I could use? To send a note up to Mr. Brunner?"

Her frown was barely perceptible as she passed me a pen and a sheet of Tropical letterhead with an envelope. I wrote on it:

> *You don't know me, I'm in town to do a certain job for you. But there's been a hitch. A serious one.*
> *Let's talk in the restaurant. Light green jacket, pale yellow tie.*
> *If this doesn't work for you, wait to be contacted by the intermediary you booked the job through.*

I didn't sign it, just folded it and inserted it in the envelope, on which I wrote "Alex Brunner" and sealed it shut. I handed it to her.

"Send it up, would you?"

"Of course," she said.

This is where, in a James Bond movie, she would have smiled at me promisingly and maybe licked her lips. But that didn't happen and, by the time she'd handed my note off to a bellboy, I'd entered the restaurant and she'd forgotten my existence.

I was assigned a booth, where another good-looking young woman who didn't give a diddly damn about me took my order for a Diet Coke. It came right away—the place really was dead—and I sat and sipped occasionally and studied the ocean, enjoying its shimmer, thinking about how good it would feel to dive into, if it weren't so fucking cold out.

Beyond a description given me by Luann, whose verbal skills were limited, Alex Brunner was a cipher to me. But he fit what she'd told me: "Big. Big belly, big head, black hair, bushy eyebrows, bushy mustache, ugly." She hadn't been wrong.

Brunner likely operated out of an office in the penthouse digs that took up the entire top floor—anyway, his predecessor had, a guy I drowned in a hot tub in a hotel, but not this hotel. Again, another story, and another monster. Just call me Van Helsing.

This guy looked like another monster, too. Features kind of blown out, like that guy in the old creature features they hired because he had acromegaly. Not quite that gross, but gross enough, tiny eyes, bulbous nose, thick lips, wealth of pock-marks. His jaunty red-with-white floral-patterned Hawaiian shirt and baggy tan surfer pants didn't make up for it. Hey, it was after business hours.

He spotted me right away. The restaurant opened off the lobby and he stood on the borderline with a couple of body-guards, also in Hawaiian shirts and surfer pants. It was like Don Ho and his backup band.

He raised a hand to them, as if he were about to take a solo, and moved past the hostess at her station without a nod or a look. She had a look for *him*, though, if behind his back—like this guy was a spoiled kid who had the run of the house and could get away with murder. Maybe literally.

"The fuck are you?" he asked. His voice was breathy and high, and it kind of spoiled the effect.

"You really want a name, Mr. Brunner?"

He slid in on the other side of the booth. His eyes were the only small feature on his big face, little black things like buttons sewn on a rag doll.

"Well?" he said.

We were in the first booth. The booths behind us were empty except for one, way down. No tables. The counter was home to a GI flirting with the waitress leaning over it on an elbow.

"I'm well aware," I said, "that I'm not supposed to contact you."

"Are you."

"But like I said in my note—there's been a hitch."

"Tell me."

"Do you know how this works?"

"How what works?"

"How somebody comes in and looks things over, and then somebody else comes in and does the job?"

His nod was slow. The sewed-on buttons became black slits.

"And how," I continued, "the somebody who looks things over, in advance, hangs around sometimes, as backup? In case help is needed?"

Another slow nod.

"Well, help was needed," I said. "Really, everything went to shit. Normally, I would just get the fuck out of Dodge. That's S.O.P."

"Is it."

"But we have a situation here. But also an opportunity."

"Do we."

"The guy I work with? Somebody on staff with the woman got wind. He and the guy I work with kinda…got into it."

"What the fuck?"

I made a face. "I'd rather not talk in here."

"It's just a restaurant, for fuck's sake."

"I hear certain people own it. Which means who knows what's wired for sound in this place? That GI over there, hitting on the cute waitress? Is he really a GI or somebody *else* who works for Uncle Sam? How 'bout that honeymoon couple toward the back? Are they really head over heels or maybe looking to fuck some heel over?"

The small black eyes had traveled to both my topics of conversation, fairly subtle about it. Now the big ugly head began to nod again, but something had changed.

"Talk about this upstairs," he said.

I wasn't anxious to do that. That penthouse would be home to those two bodyguards and, likely, more. I had something else in mind.

"Let's go out to the parking lot," I said. "Something you should see."

"Is there."

I shrugged. "You got your boys handy. It's the great out-of-doors. What's to fear?"

"I look afraid?"

"I don't know. With some people it's hard to tell. Shall we?"

He took in a bushel of air and held it a while, and when he exhaled, it was like a foul wind had come up.

"Show me," he said, sliding out and immediately looming.

Forget what I said about the high breathy voice. Actually, it came off kind of scary. This big man, big in size, big in the Dixie Mafia, might himself be the answer to, "What's to fear?"

I finished my Diet Coke, left four dollars, and led him through the pastel lobby out of his own hotel into the parking lot. The two bodyguards lingered like a bad smell as we exited into a cool night where the moon was a high-wattage affair, higher than the parking lot lighting, anyway, which seemed designed for necking and drug deals.

Just as I had with Luann, I walked him behind the LeSabre and opened the trunk and gave him a gander.

"Jesus," he said with no emotion at all.

"Here's the thing," I said, like a used car dealer demonstrating how much you could stuff in a trunk. "I wasn't the shooter. I was the stakeout dude."

He was staring at the tangle of dead men in the trunk, the plastic tarp's edges sticking up around them like frozen flames. His eyes traveled to me. "No trigger work?"

"I done my share. We'd trade off, Jimmy and me. That's Jimmy there, with the crewcut and Gandhi dot in his forehead. This other guy worked for the woman. Maybe you know him."

Brunner shook his head. He didn't. Of course he didn't.

I picked up the thread: "So, yeah sure, I can work active, which is why I'm showing you this and you aren't just hearing about it on the phone from my middleman."

"I'm listening."

I put a chummy hand on the bony boulder of a shoulder. "When I was gathering intel, I spent time in that woman's poon palace. I met her. Talked to her. Got up close and personal."

"How close? How personal?"

"Not that close. Not that personal. But enough of both for our purposes."

His forehead clenched. If he'd been thinking any harder, it

would have hurt both of us. "She don't know about this?"

"No. Her man stumbled onto Jimmy and they tangled asses, permanent. I don't figure she knows anything about it, has no idea she's a target, unless she's wondering what became of her employee here, and it's only been a few hours."

The eyes were tiny, tiny black slits now. "You could take her out?"

"You mean, would she date me?"

He just looked at me. Even Luann had a better sense of humor.

So I said, "Yeah. No problem. She thinks I'm cute. Still...it's kind of a mess."

He glanced down and grimaced, as if the smell had just registered. "Shut that thing."

"Not what I meant," I said, but I closed the trunk lid. "Look, the job got interrupted. The final payoff hadn't been made yet, as you know."

This was a bluff. Back in the Broker days, Broker would get a down payment, and—with no contact between the hit team and the client—a money drop would be arranged for a day or so before the job. Again, no contact. The client was guaranteed a refund if for some reason the job didn't go down as promised.

Brunner didn't contradict me. In fact, he said, "I have the money upstairs. I can pay you now."

"Cash?"

He nodded. "Five thousand."

"You go on up and get it. I'll wait here."

Which was my plan, part of it anyway. What I wanted was to talk this prick into fetching the money, then get him in the LeSabre and supposedly go and help dispose of the bodies. Making that part of the price of doing business. Brunner and the two in the trunk winding up a trio in a ditch in the boonies was the goal. Three peas in a blood-soaked pod.

But that wasn't coming together. And it had been a little half-assed, admittedly, and in any event Brunner wasn't playing.

"You come up," he said.

Goddamnit. This was what I got for trying to think on my feet. If I'd taken the time to dump the two bodies, I might have filled that trunk with Brunner by now. But with two dead guys in there already, there wasn't room for his fat ass.

So suddenly Brunner and I and his two bodyguards were in the elevator heading up to the eighth-floor penthouse—doing so required a key—with my expectation being to find hot-and-cold-running gun thugs. To my pleasant surprise the wood-paneled vestibule where ten years ago two hoods had been posted was empty of humanity, even of a questionable variety. Maybe these two bodyguards were the missing sentries.

But for now, at least, they followed my host and me into the suite, down a doorless hallway and into the high-ceilinged spacious living room with its walk-in kitchen off to the right. Nothing had changed, including the modern furnishings that turned their nose up at the Tropical's pastels, substituting various shades of wood and touches of dark red and dark blue.

A big-screen TV was going—*Remington Steele* was on—and the two bodyguards wandered over and took comfy chairs in front of it while that red-and-white Hawaiian shirt led me down the hall to what had once been his precursor's office.

Finally something had been remodeled, the walls a high-end dark-wood paneling now with several framed hanging items, predominantly a big watercolor of the Tropical Motel facing a *Godfather* poster. These wiseguys loved to romanticize their stupid-ass selves. Looming over a huge mahogany desk was a framed cover of *Gulf Coast Living* displaying Brunner at the wheel of a cabin cruiser, showing off a big smile that hadn't come up in our conversation so far.

He turned away as he lifted the framed magazine cover off from its hook, set it on the floor, and began working the dial on the small wall safe. He started extracting packets of money, which he tossed on the desk, five of them, each banded $1,000. Twenties, fifty per packet.

I said to his back, "Kind of a pity, dusting such a nice little piece of ass. She's no raging bitch or anything. But I suppose you got your reasons."

"She wouldn't sell out," his back said.

Then he turned and finally shared that big smile. He tossed another grand on the desk, the door to the safe still yawning open, its round mouth looking surprised by the invasion.

"For your trouble," he said.

"Thanks," I said and shot him in his left black-button eye. It took just long enough to let him register surprise before flopping onto the desk, shaking it like the deck of his cabin cruiser when he bagged a big fish. Or anyway so I supposed. I live on a lake but I don't fish.

The two bodyguards out there wouldn't have heard the cough of the silenced Browning, so I took my time looking around, though of course I kept the nine mil in one hand. I found an empty briefcase in a closet and loaded in the six packets of money, then brought out another fifteen identical $1,000 packets from that clown car of a little safe. I helped myself to some documents just because they were there. You never knew.

I left the dead man and the open safe behind, to make sure the cops read this as a robbery, and went back up the hall to the living room, where Pierce Brosnan was on the TV being debonair.

"Good show?" I asked them.

One, sitting in a Barca Lounger, shrugged, while the other in a comfy armchair, with a beer can in his fist, said, "Kinda corny." I shot them in that order, in the head. They were close enough to the picture window onto the beach to splash the windows like two big bugs had flown into it.

The same blonde was at the front desk as I exited.

I didn't rate a glance.

THREE

Luann lived on Father Ryan Avenue, one block from the beach highway, in a cozy area of small homes dating to the Depression and just before and after. Live oaks arched over sidewalks and streets, lending a spooky charm, particularly in the dead of evening. When we rolled by cross streets, the Gulf and its moon-tinged shimmer tickled the eye.

"Who was Father Ryan?" I asked her.

She was at the wheel of her brown Toyota Corolla sports coupe, which went well with that brunette hair. "A Confederate priest, my neighbor said. And a poet, too."

There was something poetic about her house, as well, when we pulled into the drive of a Spanish Mission-style place that looked like Zorro's summer cottage or anyway Don Diego's. The cream-color stucco exterior had the usual red-tile roof, parapets and carved stonework, and was taller than any one-story house had any right to be.

I have no intention of boring you with the unpleasant details of how I called Luann from a convenience store and she, expecting the call, joined me right away, leading me into the countryside to a properly secluded area to deposit the LeSabre and its surprise package in the trunk. I will only say that she pitched right in and didn't worry about getting anything unpleasant on her purple pantsuit.

Anyway, now we were entering her 1920s-era home with its plaster walls and vaulted ceilings and leaded glass windows and new furniture that ran to overstuffed chairs, Tiffany-style lamps, red-and-black flocked drapes, and other accouterments whose vaguely San Francisco whorehouse flavor might seem appropriate to someone raised as a teenage prostitute.

"I need a shower," she said, and disappeared somewhere.

I put the briefcase of money on the floor by a chaise and did the same with my overnight bag retrieved from the LeSabre. Then, like Ponce De Leon looking for the Fountain of Youth, I discovered the kitchen, a small and serviceable space all but filled by a round Formica-top table. Only a few staples were in the small refrigerator, but that included several cans of Coke, and I helped myself to one.

I sat listening to the shower drumming somewhere nearby and remembered what she looked like naked. I have a very good memory for that kind of thing. When she walked in, barefoot in an oversize emerald Chenille bathrobe, her head was lost in the big pink towel she was rubbing her hair dry with.

"You want a shower?" she asked.

"I could use one."

"You've got clean things with you, don't you?"

"I do."

She stopped toweling and looked at me with her wet hair in ropy strands, making her look like a lovely Medusa. "Go on then."

I did. I took a nice warm shower, bordering on hot, with the watery needles having their way with my aching muscles. I washed my hair and was toweling it, otherwise naked, when she stepped into the bathroom, with its art deco fixtures and subdued lighting, but she didn't have a towel.

The hourglass figure hadn't changed at all, nor the creamy complexion, not the tip-tilted handfuls with only the teasing triangle of hair different, brown now, not honey blonde. I forgave her. Visibly.

She had a crooked smile going that said maybe she did have a sense of humor after all, or maybe she was working on one.

She said, "Let's get this out of the way, shall we?"

I won't describe the bedroom to you, beyond the giant mesquite Mediterranean headboard with its forged iron straps and iron clavos. The rest is mostly a blur, though I do remember asking her if she wanted me to use something and she said no. She was on the pill. I realized birth control wasn't the only concern, well aware she'd been a hooker at an age when I was still watching *The Mickey Mouse Club*, wondering why Annette appealed to me.

But sometimes I don't play it safe and this was one of those times.

She sat me on the edge of the bed, then knelt before me as if she were praying in this mission of a house, but she wasn't. She was expert at it, starting slow and going deeper and faster and deeper, but sensing just when to stop.

Then she crawled up past me onto the bed on her back and spread her arms and her legs and the pink flower between her legs wanted plucking. I spent some time down there and she was moaning to where it almost sounded like pain.

"Enough?" I asked, looking up at her.

"Little more please. Been a long time. Gonna be tight."

"I'm okay with that."

"Little more please…"

Who was I to argue?

"Okay!" she said after a while. "Oh-kay. Should be fine. Come on, baby. Come on…"

She was tight all right but smooth and we took it slow and tender before the build-up. While I'd remembered her body, I'd forgotten how taut her nipples got and how flushed her cheeks became and how her eyes rolled back when she neared climax, and just how shudderingly, completely she would come.

I rolled off and we lay on our backs, out of breath, staring at the ceiling.

"You've been practicing," I said.

"No I haven't. I...I *tol'* you it was a long time."

"How long?"

"Since us."

I frowned at her. "What do you mean, since us?"

"Since we did it. In that room at the Tropical with the hot tub."

I rolled on my side. Leaned on an elbow. "You're kidding."

She stayed on her back. "You said I don't have a sense of humor. How could I kid?"

"Why on earth would you not...? Lovely girl like you."

She shrugged. Her nipples were soft again, nicely puffy. "Because I had my fill of fucking. I *had* to, for years and years, because that son of a bitch Mr. Woody owned me."

"But I'm different?"

"You made me come," she reminded me.

That's what she'd told me in that hot tub room after she'd been provided to me by her boss as a fuck bunny. That I was the only man who had ever made her come. I told you I was the shit.

"Baby," I said, "you don't...don't *love* me or anything, do you?"

"Don't be so full of yourself!"

I also said, if you'll recall, I might *be* a shit.

"It's just, I had my fill of staring at ceilings," she said as she stared at the ceiling. "And in my business now? All I see is how awful men are. How they think with their dicks. And paw the girls. You have any idea how many customers I've had to have my boys beat up in the parking lot?"

"I'm going to assume that's a rhetorical question."

"I don't know what that is." She glanced at me. "You want some eggs and bacon? It's all I got in the house."

I cooked the bacon and she scrambled the eggs. She was in a

purple Victoria's Secret nightie she threw on, and I was in my underwear, which was Fruit of the Loom. We were comfortable with each other. A decade ago, we spent a lot of time together. Almost a week.

"How much money you bring back in that briefcase?" she asked, not sounding like she cared all that much. All she'd asked me about Alex Brunner was, *Is he dead?*

"Twenty grand," I said.

"You take ten."

"Deal."

We ate at the Formica-topped table.

"You could stay on," she said.

"Probably not a good idea."

"Why?"

"I was seen tonight. Someone might recognize me. I was here for over a week, ten years ago. Too risky, and anyway, I don't see a strip club in my future, except maybe as a customer."

That amused her. She didn't laugh, but she smiled a little and made an unidentifiable sound at the back of her throat.

"Nobody's gonna recognize you," she said.

"Why not?"

"You're just too average."

"Thank you."

She spooned scrambled eggs. "No, really. I see a hundred like you every month."

"I can't take all this flattery."

A smirk. "I know about sarcastic now. And you are one sarcastic son of a bee."

"So I've been told. But you're right. It's part of why I'm still alive."

"What is?"

I shrugged. "That I don't look like anybody special. If a police sketch artist drew a description of me, from an eyewitness? It would look like your goddamn next-door neighbor."

"My next-door neighbor is a bald old fat guy."

"You know what I mean."

She nodded. She actually did. She'd made progress over time.

"You'll stay the night?" she asked.

"Pretty much have to. I don't have wheels. I'll have you drop me at a used car lot, someplace sleazy, in the morning."

That sounded reasonable to her.

In the living room, we went through the contents of the briefcase. She perched on the chaise and I sat, Indian-style, on the hardwood floor.

"I miscounted," I said. "It's twenty-two thousand."

"That's eleven each."

"You did get a GED."

That made her laugh. Actually made her laugh!

I was going through the documents I'd scooped up from that safe. A will, a couple of deeds, some bonds, but also two floppy disks.

"You have a computer?" I asked.

She nodded and led me to a spare bedroom that had been set up as a modest home office. She did the books here, she said. Some things couldn't get done in a backroom with a strip club out there wanting attention.

I took the chair at a little desk and she leaned in and booted the computer. Then I looked at the first floppy and brought up a list of addresses.

"I think I know what this is," I said, eyes wide, mouth yawning but in no way tired.

"What is it?"

"Jesus. These are names and addresses and, fuck, income tied to specific businesses…like Mr. Woody's."

"So?"

"Let me look at this other one." I got the other floppy going. "These names mean anything to you?"

"Cops and local politicians," she said, shrugging a little.

"Oh boy. Payoffs are listed. Names and dates and figures... shit fuck hell."

I ejected the floppy. I was seated and she was looking over my shoulder. I felt like I was a passenger in a car driven by somebody who didn't know a truck was bearing down.

"What?" she asked.

I looked at her, hard and direct. "This could put dozens of people in the slammer, my little dove. *That* floppy is the Dixie Mafia in all its glory. *This* floppy is local corruption a la mode."

"What's ice cream got to do with it?"

I stood and I held her by the biceps, gentle but firm. "You have a choice," I said.

"Like you did, when you had to decide whether to kill me or not, that time?"

I shook my head. "That choice was nothing compared to this. These computer disks can get you killed or they could make you rich, or anyway get you killed trying to get rich. So you have options."

Her face remained blank. I might have told her the grass needed cutting. "What are they?"

"You could give them to the FBI."

She frowned, just a little. "That's what would get me killed."

"One of the ways. You could sell them to whoever's the most powerful person on each disk—there's no overall Dixie Mafia boss, but you probably know which one or two or three hold the most sway."

"But they might say they'd pay me and then kill me instead."

"Right. Or you could destroy those fucking floppies and forget all about them. *I* forgot about them already."

"No you didn't."

"You'd be surprised." I nodded toward the disks. "I want nothing to do with the things."

Her frown deepened. "You think I should just get rid of them?"

"Blackmail is always a bad idea. The worst idea is blackmailing those people individually."

"Why?"

"Some would play along, but all it would take is for one to say the hell with it, and torture you till you give the disks up and then…"

She nodded. "Kill me."

"Right. And I don't have to tell you that there are some terrible people out there willing to kill other people for money."

We didn't speak of it again. In the morning we skipped breakfast—we'd already had bacon and eggs last night—and she drove me to a different used car lot where I spent a grand and change from my share of the briefcase money on a green 1975 Mustang with enough tire tread to get me back to Wisconsin. I kissed her, and it was kind of sweet, but as I headed out of Biloxi, I was afraid for her.

But I didn't find out what choice she'd made until much later.

2021

FOUR

Both wives died on me, but only one by gunfire.

Linda had been a sweet kid, not terribly bright, though as sexy and fun as you could ever want, yet able to just sit quietly and keep me company when I wasn't in the mood to talk. That sweet time didn't last long, because my efforts to be part of the straight world got interrupted when my past caught up to me, turning Linda into collateral damage and leaving me to pick up the pieces. And kill the people responsible, of course.

But my life on Paradise Lake in Wisconsin, where I'd bought into Wilma's Welcome Inn and managed it, too, had to be left behind. I'd made one of my rare excursions into a bottle—I'm really not much of a drinker, but some situations just call for it—before by luck or happenstance or maybe fate running into an old friend who'd also been in the resort business in the Great Lakes. Gary Petersen, who I'd known in Vietnam where we were both Marines, was running Sylvan Lodge in Minnesota and had over-extended himself with a second property and needed a manager who knew the ropes.

I had qualified and wound up on Sylvan Lake, where in the off-season I looked after the facility with just a little help from José, a maintenance guy, two days a week. I was good with people but it was a skill I exercised only by necessity, enjoying the months alone far more. For a long while I had a cabin on the lake that was a lot like my old A-frame on Paradise Lake. A short jog across the highway took me to our fitness center with indoor pool and sauna and workout area, and these kept me in shape as the years slipped by and the straight life swallowed me back up.

Then about fifteen years ago I got briefly pulled back into my old profession—that "one last job" you hear so much about and that often gets a guy killed. But a boatload of money was on offer, and after so many hits, what was left of my conscience wouldn't be taxed by one more. Only my target turned out to be a nice young woman named Janet Wright, who just didn't seem like the kind of person anybody would want to kill, and before long that included me.

Romantic, huh? The "Wright" girl coming along? It was sunshine, lollipops and roses, if you're okay with me ridding the world of everybody who wanted her dead and marrying the girl. Janet inherited controlling interest in a Chicago media empire that included a superstation, selling out for several million, which meant I wound up making more money by *not* killing her.

She was a librarian, Janet, but the kind of librarian *Playboy* used to love to search out to have lay down her books and let down her hair and take off her glasses and everything else and make a man's mouth water. She was funny and smart, but, like Linda, knew when to just be quiet and sit with me looking at the lake, or read a book by Joyce Carol Oates on her side of the bed while I read a Louis L'Amour on mine.

With her money, we bought Gary out when that big good-natured grizzly said he wanted to retire to Florida with his tiny wife Ruth. We took over a two-story cedar-sided cabin no bigger than Tara, a condo that we'd been renting out to rich people before we were rich people. Our life after that was quiet and we spoiled ourselves rotten. We worked hard but a lot of people who worked for us worked harder.

The off-seasons, however, reverted to me looking after the lodge and José's son Manny and two helpers doing all the maintenance. Janet liked to cook, but we would also drive to nearby

Brainerd where half a dozen restaurants did the cooking for us. I liked to tinker with my 1977 black Firebird, until getting in and out of it threatened to require me to phone for the jaws of life; we replaced it with a silver Cadillac SUV. We even took vacations, seeing London and Paris and Rome.

Considering what a violent fucked-up Vietnam vet I'd been for a good thirty years, these last fifteen, more like sixteen, had been quiet and goddamn idyllic. A far better happy ending than I deserved.

I kept guns all around the place tucked here and there where I could get at them—something Janet approved of, knowing all there was to know about me, including that I'd once been hired to kill her. This indicates that all through those quiet years I knew a loud knock could come to the door and authorities finally find me, or a back door could have its lock picked with my security system disabled and my past could once again come looking for me. If it did, I was not about to let this wife, the goddamn fucking love of my life, be collateral damage, too.

And then Covid got her.

Maybe there's an irony in that. A librarian who was a voracious reader of more than westerns could have found it, if there was any. To me, I just saw something strangely fitting about a killer more deadly than yours truly coming out of nowhere to snuff out the life of a sweet, gentle woman who had given me the happiest decade and a half of my life.

She didn't suffer much. It was, like some asshole said once, like the flu in her case, except that on day three of it she died. No intensive care or respirator, which was as close to a blessing as came out of it.

That had been five months ago. This time I didn't retreat into a bottle. What I did was fall back into the quiet lifestyle I'd shared with Janet, though certain elements were missing. I'd eased or perhaps slid back into an even more solitary existence than before I'd met either of my better halves.

No more poker games with buddies in Brainerd, though I did head across the highway to the fitness center and swim every day and work out some. No more restaurants, not even the Sylvan Lodge dining room until recently, because it had been closed during the pandemic; but I drove into Brainerd once a month to the gun range to keep up my skills, because you never know.

No more picking up waitresses and college girls and divorcees for sex and some sense of human contact. I was past that now. Too old. For my age, and for having had a double bypass, I was in good shape, no paunch, muscles hard here, ropy there. I took pills in the morning, but not many. My knees used to be better, but they were working. My hair was steel gray. There had been times when I went bearded, but not now. I didn't need to look older, despite my boyish countenance.

I would be seventy soon.

Someone knocked at the door.

Seated mid-room in an overstuffed brown leather recliner facing a 4K 55" TV above the hearth of a formidable fieldstone fireplace, in which a gas fire was going, I switched off the Audie Murphy western (*No Name on the Bullet*) I'd been watching on TCM.

Wind was whistling outside because winter was here, and snow, too, although it wasn't snowing right now. Mid-afternoon, the sun was under clouds but up there somewhere, hiding like a fugitive. One side of the two-story great room (as Janet called it) was lined with floor-to-ceiling windows. That provided a postcard look past the deck onto Lake Sylvan, which was frozen over, wearing winter-ravaged trees along the surrounding shoreline like a crown of thorns, providing an austere landscape as a backdrop for whoever had come calling.

But the door someone had rapped their knuckles on was not glass—it was over to the right and as wooden as a cigar-store Indian. I make that comparison to prove I am almost seventy.

I waited to see if the knock repeated. If it was cops, either a loud voice or a battering ram would follow. My hand slipped between the armrest of the recliner and the cushion I was seated on. It brought back a nine-millimeter Browning that I had owned for decades.

Going to the nearest of the windows, I could get an angle on my caller—a slender woman plumped up by a shiny black puffy parka with a light brown fur collar framing an oval face obscured by dark-lens sunglasses with oversized cat-eye frames. She wore black ribbed pants under which combat boots lurked, an over-size bag over one shoulder. She looked like somebody in an Eskimo fashion show.

She knocked again.

I opened the door with my left hand, the nine mil in my right tucked behind my back. She smiled. Her lipstick was a startling red emphasized by the blinding white of her teeth.

"Mr. Keller?" she asked.

I said nothing. My face also said nothing.

She began to offer a black-gloved hand, thought better of it, and gestured to herself instead. "Susan Breedlove. I'm a writer—a true crime writer. Perhaps you've heard of me?"

My face and I again said nothing.

"I've written several *New York Times* bestsellers—*The Case Against Casey Anthony*? *Unabomber—Profile in Madness*?"

I began to close the door and she whipped off her sunglasses. Her eyes were big and blue, with no eye makeup, unless those spiky eyelashes had been aided and abetted. She leaned in.

"Look," she said, her breath pluming from the pretty red gash that was her mouth, "it's cold out here—could I please come in?"

I was getting cold myself. I shrugged in a what-the-hell manner and let her in, shoving the nine mil in my waistband in back. I was in black sweats, by the way. If you think that was because I'd been exercising across the way earlier, you're wrong. I was just a house-bound lazy old fuck.

She took off her gloves and stuffed them in the pockets of her coat, which she seemed to want me to help her out of, so I did and hung it over a nearby chair. Her light gray turtleneck managed to be loose and clingy at once. She was tiny and reminded me a little of Luann in Biloxi, in her white-blonde days; this girl—no, young woman (she looked to be in her thirties, maybe early forties)—was similarly petite and curvy.

"I would kill," she said, wandering into the great room with its rustic-looking but expensive furnishings, "for something warm. Coffee. Tea. Cocoa. Anything."

I followed her. "You have your nerve—give you that."

She shrugged, hugged herself. It *was* a little cold, even inside. "Well, if I waited for you to be hospitable, I might freeze to death first."

She strolled around the big room and paused at the field-stone fireplace, facing its warmth. Her eyes lifted to travel the open beams.

"Lovely place," she said.

"So glad you approve."

I nodded her toward the overstuffed couch next to the recliner, where I sat, keeping the chair in its upright, slightly rocking position. She settled on the near end of the couch, her handbag's strap still over one shoulder. The fire wasn't as warm as a wood-burning one would be, but it sufficed and the flames added the proper orange-blue ambiance.

"If you're who I think you are," Susan Breedlove said, "you know why I'm here."

"Do I?"

The big blue eyes regarded me unblinkingly. "Are you him?"

"….'Him'?"

She shivered, from the chill maybe, then shrugged in a way that brought her shoulders all the way up to the bottom of her ears before going back down. "If so, I'm in danger…I get that. That's why my secretary and several business associates know this was my destination. But that's *all* they know. Just enough for you to have to hear me out before you decide if the risk is worth it."

"Worth it for what?"

"What else? Killing me."

I said nothing.

She said, "You know, I've tried to tally it up, but it's really hard. In the circles you traveled in, in your day, the types you bumped heads with were pretty free with violence themselves. But I think it's easily over thirty, or maybe as many as forty. And that doesn't include Vietnam, of course."

I stood.

She put a hand on the shoulder bag. A gun in there. That was obvious.

I said, "I'm not a coffee drinker, but I can make you tea. Or hot chocolate."

She relaxed, just a little, though her hand remained on the bag. Smiled, barely. "You're a Diet Coke man, aren't you?"

"Not when it's this cold. Hot chocolate. Want some?"

"Please. Easy on the marshmallows. Watching my figure."

"Like the men around you."

"You *are* him."

I played it casual. "Frankly, I don't know what you're talking about. But this is off-season and I'm bored and you're attractive, so why not indulge you? Not a lot of authors stop by."

"*Fellow* authors, you mean?"

I got up to get her the hot chocolate, knowing she'd see the nine mil stuffed in the back of my waistband. Let her chew on that with that pretty mouth. Fuck casual.

I delivered the hot chocolate and she took the cup with an appreciative nod. I had brought along a cup for myself, too, and returned to the recliner.

"You've accused me of multiple murders," I said, "and now you imply I'm an author? Isn't murderer bad enough?"

She sipped hot chocolate. A little smudge of white marshmallow lingered on her red upper lip. Get your head out of the gutter.

My guest said, "You wrote four novels that appeared from a paperback publisher in the mid-seventies. You did one more, ten years later, for a different house. Those books gave you away, despite the lengths you'd gone to, to change names and places."

"Did they really?"

She nodded, her pink tongue disposing of the stray marshmallow fleck. "Those 'fictional' accounts had strong parallels to real events I came across through general true-crime research. I searched copyright, but it belonged to someone who disappeared in the 1980s. I tried to track down your editors, but both were dead by the time I discovered who they were."

"I have an alibi for those," I said.

She ignored that. "Natural causes in both cases. But those novels were my guide. I called *my* book *Sniper—The Killer Who Came Home*. From Vietnam?"

I gave her a one-shoulder shrug, sipped my hot chocolate. "I read westerns mostly. You say you write nonfiction based on novels? Isn't that backwards?"

She set her cup on a coaster on the end table between us. "Well, they were published as novels, but we both know they're *memoirs*, don't we, Jack?…May I call you that? It's what you use here, and you've actually used that first name fairly often, haven't you?"

"Give me your purse."

She swallowed and hot chocolate had nothing to do with it.

I gestured with four curled summoning fingers.

She handed it over.

I opened the handbag and, among all the female stuff, there snuggled a Baby Glock.

So Susan Breedlove, true-crime writer, packed a nine mil, too—a Glock 26 that fired the same cartridges as my Browning. But there was no digital recorder, her phone wasn't recording either, and her I.D. looked legit. She was 45. A bit older than I'd thought. Nothing too surprising, What I didn't expect to see was that she lived in Davenport, Iowa.

The Broker had worked out of Davenport.

"Take off your clothes," I told her.

She seemed to think that was a joke at first, but my expression said otherwise.

"Stand by the fire," I said, "so you don't get too cold."

She got to her feet, stood with her back to the fireplace, and stripped down, combat boots and all. Her body was nice, shapely but muscular enough to indicate she worked out, too. Her breasts were full and not at all droopy, age treating her well so far. Her pubic patch was trimmed way back, but she was a natural blonde. The backlighting of the fire made the front of her almost a silhouette, but not quite.

"You see a wire?" she asked, arms and hands spread in a "preeeesenting" fashion, letting the irritation and indignity show. She gestured to the pile of clothing at her feet. "May I put these back on?"

"Please."

She did, as hurriedly as if she had a bus to catch. Icily, she said, "If you're not aware of my book, I should tell you that everything vital about your past is revealed, including your real name, family history, military record…with many of the probable contract killings linked to you…somewhat speculatively, I grant you. Again, thanks to those paperbacks. Even with names and places changed, they were a tremendous help, a guide. I really should have shared my royalties with you…and if you hadn't made me strip, I still might've."

"Assuming you're not insane," I said, "which I am not ready to concede…what do you want from me?"

She sighed. Returned to where she'd been sitting and rested her hands on her clad-again knees. "Your cooperation. You see, I'm…I'm writing a sequel."

"*What?*"

"A sequel," she said, chin up, "and it's your fault."

"*My* fault?"

She nodded defensively. "You had dropped off the face of the earth…even the copyright office lost track of you. But then, about fifteen years ago, you started in again."

I grunted a laugh. "What, killing people?"

"Quite the opposite. Writing again. In your retirement, I suppose. Another round of paperbacks, more of them this time. Stories about contracts you carried out in the early seventies. Not so fussy about changing places—names yes, places no. You also did other books about your using the Broker's list, as you call it, to become a hitman who hit hitmen…sounds silly, putting it that way, doesn't it?"

But she hadn't said "the Broker"—she used his real *name, which I had never shared with anyone. Including you.*

"Your current editor stonewalls me," she said. "Claims the books are delivered through circuitous means."

"Good. Then I guess I won't have to kill him."

"I promise to protect you," she said, hands folded now, very schoolgirl, painfully sincere. "I already have enough research done to write a second book. But if you would *help* me…sit for an interview in depth…with your identity concealed, never to be disclosed…we could both get very rich."

"I'm rich enough."

She shrugged indifferently. "I'm doing okay myself, but who couldn't use more money? You can't have been doing well during Corona. And you wouldn't have to fire a shot. Of course, I would imagine it's been a while since you fired a shot, outside of a firing range."

A part of my brain that had gone to sleep fifteen or sixteen years ago woke up and started thinking about killing this foolish young woman.

I rose. "This is fascinating, but you have the wrong man…. Though it's interesting to see how you people work."

She looked up at me with an offended face. "You *people?*"

"Supermarket tabloid journalists. 'I Had Hitler's Child,' 'The Vampire Baby Sucked My Blood.' If you want another hot chocolate, I'll fix you up with a plastic to-go cup."

I gave the purse back to her, with the little Browning inside. Immediately she dug her hand in there and, thinking I'd misjudged the situation, I slipped my hand behind me to the coolness of the Browning grip.

But all she did was fish out a business card.

Stiffening, she held it out and said, "If I'm wrong about you, I apologize. But I'm not wrong, am I? Making me strip like that…that was so *Quarry….*"

"Quarry?"

"Don't bother." She flew to her feet. "If you change your mind about working with me, Jack, that number is where to find me. But you should know—I'm going to do the book with or without you."

She went to the chair near the door where I'd hung her

puffy black coat and got into it, a bear skin rug reclaimed by its rightful owner. She got her gloves on, her purse on the strap over her shoulder as she looked back at me.

"Oh," she said, nothing phony about it at all, "and I'm very sorry about your wife. I know how much you loved her. I lost an aunt to Covid."

She went out, closing the door behind her.

I stared at that door for a long time—at least thirty seconds, which is longer than it sounds. Then I went down the hall to my home office, a bedroom we'd converted. My desk and computer and a file cabinet and a bunch of bookcases were in there, the smallest room in the house that wasn't a bath. One bookcase was filled with multiple copies of my ill-advised "novels." Couldn't I have come up with a better hobby, like putting pins in butterflies or killing deer with a bow and arrow?

I went to the shelf nearest my desk, where various reference books were handy, and from there took my copy of *Sniper—The Killer Who Came Home*. The dust jacket was tattered, though the book was only a few years old, and the book itself had seen a lot of wear. Many pages had been dog-eared in the reading and re-reading.

I studied the author's picture on the flyleaf of the dust jacket —Susan Breedlove, a little younger, very pretty but not smiling, since this was a book about a merciless killer, after all. Her bio didn't mention Davenport, Iowa.

Yes, I knew her the moment I saw her on my doorstep.

And I had already read her fucking book.

FIVE

I tried to sleep that night, and failed. The tossing and turning, and my buzzing brain, sent me back to my recliner and the flat-screen TV, but nothing interested me. So many channels, a wise man once said, and nothing on.

So it was three A.M. when I rolled my swimsuit up in a towel, got back in my sweats, grabbed my ring of keys, and hefted my Browning nine millimeter in preparation for a visit to the resort's fitness center. It had been a long time since I'd felt the need for a firearm to accompany me for a relaxing swim, but having Susan Breedlove, author of *Sniper*, drop by had unsettled the fuck out of me.

I threw on the forest-green fleece-lined, vaguely military jacket with multiple pockets that Janet got me for Christmas two years ago, snugged the nine mil in a nice deep pocket and my key ring in another, and tucked the towel under my left arm. Then I put the jacket's hood up and went out the back way, cutting over to the lane that ran through a wooded area between my overgrown cabin and the three-story resort.

Cabins nestled along the lake in those woods off a little sub-lane shooting off from the main one; but those cabins were uninhabited this time of year, so nothing lit up the trees like oversize fireflies, as happened when tourists were here. The sleeping behemoth of the resort had only a few lights on, timer-generated ones that went from this main-floor room to that one like a slow-moving ghost.

As I trotted along, the cold air had a bite but not much wind to back it up, and a chunk of moon and plenty of stars made the night unusually clear. The snow had a crust with a sparkle when the moonlight hit it. Normally this would have provided a peaceful ambiance. Tonight it was more in the quiet-too-quiet category.

I ambled across the empty two lanes that separated the resort from the fitness center. José and his son had plowed the little parking lot, kind of a pointless effort this time of year. I worked the key in the door, which I locked behind me, and adjusted the dimmer switch on the lights to get away from the default family fun lighting and create something more like dusk.

The big vertical room was lined with windows on both sides, but the view was mostly more trees, so beautifully encrusted with ice that they looked phony. Wood tables and chairs lined one side of the Olympic-size pool and beach chairs the other, for those who thought an indoor pool in Minnesota was the beach.

There'd be no workout in the wee hours with weights, no riding the stationary bike, no treadmill. Just swim and a sauna. I stripped down and get into my trunks—way past the age for a Speedo—and, with no small children around to frighten, exposed my various bullet, knife and surgical scars to the muggy air. I kept the pool warm when I was the only one around to use it.

At the far end, past the weights and other workout gear, was the box-like sauna with seating for maybe half a dozen sweating souls. I went in and turned on the heater at a setting that, within forty-five minutes, would give me the desired 165F. Even after all this time, all these years, the pine smell made me smile.

A good trick tonight.

Back in the big echo chamber, I dove into the pool—there's a diving board but I never use it—and swam lazy laps for maybe half an hour. I didn't think of anything. Not a goddamn thing. What I like most about swimming is how conducive it is to not thinking, but (paradoxically) also to thinking. And when the laps were done, I floated on my back and looked at the water reflect off the ceiling, making shadows that drifted and shapes that turned into other shapes. But unlike a kid making animals out of clouds, I didn't see anything but abstract forms trying unsuccessfully to mean something. The thoughts that wormed their way in, however, were concrete.

The Breedlove woman had got a lot right in her book. She'd tracked me down as far as my hometown and folks and schooling —I lettered in swimming, which should come as no surprise to you—and also my military record. Two tours in Vietnam, much of it as a sniper, winning a Bronze star if you call that winning, and so on.

She knew that I'd come home and found the wife I'd married shortly before leaving for Nam in bed with a mechanic named Williams. I've always been a little proud that I didn't kill that prick immediately, and I wouldn't have killed him at all if, the next day, he hadn't looked up at me from under the sports-car he was working on to call me a bunghole. That, more than anything, was why I kicked out the jack.

And of course there in California a lot of publicity had been generated—La Mirada wasn't a big town, still isn't—and I'd made headlines when the preliminary hearing led to charges being dropped. I was just enough of a war hero to get some folks riled up in my favor, after which I became just enough of a pariah to be unemployable.

She'd been on the money with the Broker's side of things, how he had been the agent, the middleman, through whom I got my jobs for the five years I spent doing contract killings. He was very smooth, the Broker—like somebody who walked out of a liquor ad. Remember that old-time Hollywood actor, Franchot Tone? Paste a mustache on him and you're there. He found me when I was on my first bender, in a cheap pad in L.A., where he told me that he could arrange for me to do what I did for chump change in Vietnam for real money in the Good Old USA.

Let's get something straight. I'm not a psychopath or a sociopath. I'm somebody your tax dollars trained in killing people and I got good at it, including the part where you aren't emotional about something that's preordained. By which I mean, by the time I got a contract, the party targeted not to be alive had already been deemed dead. So what did I have to do with it?

Breedlove in her book sort of theorized about that point of view, and my "Post Traumatic Stress Disorder" and how I must have "rationalized" things, because people she talked to said I seemed to be a decent, nice, normal kind of young man.

Well, I was a decent, nice, normal old man now, wasn't I? So why couldn't she leave me alone? I hadn't killed anybody in fifteen, sixteen years!

The only way she'd known about the Broker's list—his database, you'd call it now—was my own goddamn books. If I had it to do over again, I wouldn't publish the fucking things. But we were—and are—way past that now....

Breedlove—in writing her sniper book—had only been able to work from what she could extrapolate from the handful of paperbacks I'd written about the list in the mid-'70s. If I hadn't started writing these memoirs again, she wouldn't know about the years I spent helping people who'd been earmarked for death.

Of course, if she wrote that second book, maybe she'd rehabilitate my image. Does a guy with PTSD go around helping people, getting rid of the assassins sent after them and identifying, sometimes removing, the person who wants them dead? If you were on somebody's hit list, wouldn't you appreciate my help?

Sure you would.

As I floated there, watching shadowy liquid shapes try to form into something but not succeeding, I wondered if I should actually consider cooperating with her on a follow-up. After all, she'd had a lot of success with *Sniper* and it hadn't come back on me at all.

Of course, I'd been amused and irritated that there'd been a movie and, briefly, a highly inaccurate television series that made me out to be some kind of humorless jerk. And still none of it had led anybody to me. Of course, I hadn't made any money off it, either, which was a crock.

But going along with a sequel? That was madness. Insanity. Just because the first book hadn't touched me, the next one damn well might.

And she knew who I was in my current life. Where I lived. She had looked right at me and I had looked right at her.

The reality was I had two options.

I could pack up and grab my getaway money and find someplace else to be. With Janet not here, what would I be walking away from, anyway? A hell of a lot, actually—all of my money, Janet's money and mine, was tied up in Sylvan Lodge. Did I want to be a seventy-year-old man living on a phony I.D. somewhere? Trying to make a few hundred thousand in squirreled-away cash last the rest of a lifetime?

Or…I could kill her.

That didn't appeal to me. She was a civilian. She was smart and likeable and good-looking. She had nerve, too, coming right at me like that. Bearding the lion in his den. Still, she *had* come at me—waded into my life, unbidden. If you get an idea to walk through a swamp, don't be surprised if a copperhead bites you.

I swam over to the side and crawled out. Toweled off at the table where my jacket was slung over a chair. Towel wrapped around me like a sarong, I padded over to the sauna booth and slipped inside. The warmth, no, the heat, enveloped me, and was at once calming, slowing the cascading thoughts. I ladled some water onto the black rocks atop the little stove, then, as steam rose lazily, climbed up onto the upper softwood bench and let the heat and pine aroma penetrate.

I didn't want to give up this life. I really didn't. Even without Janet in it, this was what I had—solitary comfort and a financial cushion and memories that weren't tied up with killing. Whether I deserved it wasn't an issue. I would get what I deserved soon enough, which was to go back to the black void from which I emerged at birth. It's what we all get, and the vast nothingness out there doesn't care whether we deserve it or not.

But was I ready to send a young woman like Susan Breedlove into that nothingness to preserve what I had for a few more fucking years? Maybe. Christ knew I'd done worse.

All the swimming in an Olympic pool and sweating in a sauna wouldn't answer much less remedy any of this. Maybe it was time for one last crawl into a bottle. Maybe the third time would be the charm.

I slipped off the top bench and came down from the lower one to switch off the stove, but halted before I did, thinking maybe I heard something. Or had I sensed it? You didn't hear much in here from that outer area, unless kids were screaming and doing cannonballs or something. And I was alone.

Wasn't I?

The only window in the pine box—and that I was in a pine

box is an irony not lost on me—took up the top half of the door, and always got steamed over. I slipped the towel off, still in my trunks (almost dry now), and rubbed a small viewing circle in one corner of that window. Had a look.

Someone had just stepped into the fitness center from out-side, and I was pretty sure he wasn't a guest of the Sylvan Lodge.

He was of medium size, black pullover sweater and black gloves and black jeans and black sneakers and black balaclava, a goddamn wintertime ninja. He was fanning around another black item: an automatic pistol. Even at this distance, I recog-nized it: a Browning Black Label 1911, probably a .22. That was the caliber many in my former profession preferred, although I was a nine-millimeter man myself.

Or had been.

He moved slowly but deliberately along the side of the pool where my jacket was slung over the back of a wooden chair at a wooden table. You remember my jacket, don't you? The vaguely military-like one with all the pockets? One of which had my fucking nine mil in it?

At my jacket he paused, but he didn't take time to go through it, not that it improved my situation any.

He moved right along, making his stealthy but calculated way toward the sauna. I just knew his next move would be to check this booth, and that he'd likely come in shooting, sending an arc of bullets around indiscriminately if thoroughly.

He was about my size and yet he was Goliath and I was David when I kicked the door open and flung the hot rock in a sling fashioned from my towel. The mini-boulder struck him in the forehead and knocked him onto the hard tile floor on his back. The pistol fired as he did this, the slug careening off weight-bench metal, then I was stomping on his throat with my bare right foot. As he choked helplessly, I picked up the Browning .22 (I'd been right, that's what it was) and for one second I considered questioning him, then shot him in the head.

I stood there panting. Goddamnit, I was old! A few feet from that sauna and I was out of breath? What the fuck? I knelt and yanked off the balaclava, lifting his head, which then set itself down with a clunk as I regarded a face that hadn't lived very long yet stared up at the shadow-drifting ceiling with eyes that had already seen too much. Those eyes were dark brown, the hair black and military short. He was white and his features had a boyish cast.

I might have been looking at my own reflection, fifty years ago, only fifty years ago I wouldn't have been stupid enough to get killed like this. Blood pooled under his head, but not much. His heart wasn't pumping the stuff, so the blessing here, besides me still breathing, was the mess would be minimal.

But shit! I had a dead body on my hands.

I searched him. He had a black leather holster on his hip, empty of course. In his right pocket was a spare magazine of .22 cartridges, and in his left a car-key fob and a little pouch of lock picks, which he'd obviously utilized to get in here. He had not fouled himself upon dying and for this I thanked him.

But the lack of any clue as to who he might have been working with made me curse him. It was possible he was a lone wolf, but back in the day we worked active and passive, and I figured that hadn't changed: somewhere out there was a surveillance guy who also provided backup. The passive member of the team might not have hung around for the hit itself, but that was relatively rare.

And my instincts, my reflexes, were undoubtedly less than they'd been fifteen or sixteen years ago. Yet I could sense him out there.

Where?

They would have been told who they were dealing with. That I wasn't just some old fart puttering around an off-season resort. Well, I was, but I was an old fart who used to kill people for a living and—I will say immodestly—one who had achieved something of a reputation.

Would the stakeout guy have flown already, his job done? Or was he still in the area, waiting for a call? Could he be outside somewhere, providing backup should the old boy turn out to be frisky?

I quickly got dressed, right down to the military-style coat of many pockets, leaving my nine mil in its pocket and filling my right hand with the dead kid's .22. I had a corpse to dispose of, yes, but he wasn't going anywhere, and nobody but me was around.

Except maybe this kid's negligent chaperone.

I thought it through. Since Janet's death, I had rarely left the condo and then only to take a meal in a restaurant in Brainerd, which had been only twice in the last three weeks and on different days of the week. I'd gone to only one movie, the new James Bond. As for swimming and working out, I had no set schedule, although this was the first time in maybe two months I'd hit the fitness center at night. A morning or afternoon was more usual.

Leaving so infrequently, and at such disparate times, made me an erratic subject. And here in the dead world of the Sylvan Lodge could that surveillance have been undertaken without me noticing?

But in any event, a stakeout would come away with the likelihood that I could best be dealt with at home, late at night, when I was asleep. Only when the kid in black had come calling, the lights had been on in the fitness center building and he had changed his plans.

I went out the back, through where supplies were stored—

had this kid and his probable partner known what they were doing, they'd have come in that way. I moved through the trees around to the highway, the fitness center's small parking lot at my back, the resort like a beached ocean liner across the way— no sign of any vehicle on the shoulder of the highway or in the side parking lot.

But in the rear lot waited a single solitary car, a nondescript gray Chevy Impala, ten or fifteen years old. The fob unlocked it. I used my gloved hands to have a look inside. For an old buggy, it was clean as a whistle. Nothing in it at all…

…except for the cell phone on the rider's seat.

I got out of the Impala and trotted back over to the fitness center. The dead kid was waiting patiently for me by the pool. I knelt and pressed his right forefinger to the phone's fingerprint reader and unlocked it.

I checked the call history and the same number turned up the last half dozen times. Then I stood there with the phone in my palm, knowing that it had the answers I needed but being too much of an old man to know how to ask it the right questions. There was probably a map in here, and a record of locations visited, and some kind of GPS I could use to track the number the kid had called six times. If *Janet* were here…

But she wasn't.

Anyway, the backup guy, also much younger than me undoubtedly, would likely be pro enough to keep his phone clean of such techie things on a job. But this was not the backup guy's phone, was it? Though it might lead me to him.

Think, dipshit, my brain said.

They'd been staking me out. Where the hell from? The dead kid hadn't been working surveillance, but the other guy almost certainly would have shared with the shooter photos of the target's house and comings and goings.

Grinning to myself, feeling marginally less a dipshit, I went through the photos on the phone. And it was a memory book of sorts of my recent several weeks—shots of me leaving the house, at the wheel of my car heading up the lane, coming back down the lane, walking across to the fitness center, and so on. Even a shot today of Susan Breedlove parking next to my car alongside the condo and another on the deck, knocking at my door.

Though it was a vast assortment, a virtual array of images chronicling the boring life I'd been leading, the majority of the photos were from the same angle. It didn't take much study to figure from what vantage point most of these photos had been taken.

I walked across the highway, so little traveled this time of year, and headed toward my condo. But when I approached it, I cut over on the lane into the woodsy area where cabins were inter-spersed along the lake—uninhabited cabins, this time of year.

Mostly uninhabited.

I walked along the left side of the lane, hugging the trees. I could see fine, a combination of night vision and moonlight fil-tering through the canopy of trees in a dappled, eerie manner. At the first of the rustic little numbers—each was separated generously from its neighbor by not just a surrounding yard but trees on either side—I paused and compared the view from here to the ones frequently turning up on the confiscated phone. Sometimes the views of the condo or me behind the wheel were closer, as if taken from the trees and not the sub-lane; but almost always from this approximate angle.

The cabins were set up with their backs to the lake, their front doors facing the lane, each with a mini-deck and few wooden steps up from a small gravel apron. My running shoes made no sound, not even a squeak, as I climbed those steps to the small deck. The phone was in my left hand, my thumb poised to ring the dead kid's favorite number. I figured it would either literally ring or be on silent mode. But if the backup man was here—and he might not be, as I'd spotted no car—he would probably be waiting for a call from his partner.

As for the lack of a vehicle, they had likely traveled together. I rarely had done that with my partners in the killing game, but not everybody works the same way. It's an individualistic trade.

Positioned with my back to one side of the outer wall by the front door, I thumbed the little phone image and, soon, heard the ring—nothing cute, just the standard default setting, not loud, but I could hear it, all right.

He responded quick, a revolver limp at his side, talking as he burst outside: "You back already?"

I slammed the flat of the .22 barrel into his forehead and he stumbled back inside and sat down hard on the wood floor, the revolver tumbling from his fingers and well out of reach. He was plump and maybe forty, with a shaved head and a full-face beard; he was wearing a black-and-white plaid shirt and chinos and work boots, an outdoorsman look in case anybody spotted him around here, maybe.

A hand went to his forehead like he was checking his temperature; a gash wept blood. I shut the door with a backward kick. Around us, like ghosts, were the sheet-covered furnishings of the off-season cabin. A space heater and an inflatable mattress and a small portable fridge were packed up in the middle of the room. A small suitcase was snapped shut and ready to go, as the job was nearly over, right? A few odds and ends waited to be loaded up separately—a gas lantern that had given him enough light to read by but nothing that would make the windows glow and tip his presence, a laptop, a pair of field glasses like he was a fucking bird watcher or something.

"You're him," the passive guy said, jaw dropping like a trap door.

"If by 'him,'" I said, "you mean the son of a bitch you came to kill, yeah, I'm him. What's your name?"

"Do you need my name? What good does it do you?"

No more than it would be doing him soon.

I asked him, "Would you like to live?"

He said nothing. Just swallowed. He had cow eyes. Brown ones. He was thinking about crying. Blood from the gash on his forehead was dripping over his eyebrows.

"It's not a rhetorical question," I said. "Would…you…like… to…live?"

"Of course I would like to live."

"Then I want the name of your broker."

"My what?"

Times had changed.

I sighed and said, "The middleman. The conduit between you and the client."

He swallowed thickly. "I don't know who the client is. I have no idea who the client is."

"Right. But the middleman does. Your agent."

He grimaced. Blood was streaking his face now. "That's not how it works."

He was telling *me* how it works? Of course, it had been a while.

"How does it work?" I asked.

He shrugged. "It's all online. Larry and me never met who we get the jobs through. Started with a couple thousand dollars, cash, each, showing up in the mail."

"Why would you and Larry get money sent to you by a stranger?"

"We were both in Afghanistan. We both won a bunch of medals. We both…"

"Killed a lot of towel heads?"

"We never called them that."

"Sure you did. I don't. But you did."

The bleeding had stopped, but when he shook his head, what was already there whipped around. "I have nothing to give you. The email address changes all the time. I don't think Bill fucking Gates could track it. God knows I'd like to help you, mac."

" 'Mac.' Does that mean you know I was a Marine?"

"Yeah, I knew that. I knew we needed to be careful, even if…"

"I'm older than sin?"

He nodded. "Look, I was a Marine, too."

I shot him in the head.

SIX

I'm not proud of myself for what came next.

I left the bald backup guy on the cabin floor and exited into the chill of the night, shutting the door on him and walking across the little deck to sit at the top of the steps. The reality of having two corpses on my hands overwhelmed me—I'd had my old life hurled at me into this new one. Like I was the barn and all the shit getting thrown at me was sticking.

Only in a way this *wasn't* my new life, not really. Yes, for a decade and a half I'd followed the straight and narrow path. But now I was just another grieving husband who lost his wife to that fucking plague. I will admit to tears when I lost Janet. That's all I'm going to give you about it, but you can have that much.

So I sat there and felt sorry for myself for a good thirty seconds. No, that's wrong—more like I felt troubled. It shook me that I felt shaken.

Then I said, "Fuck it," and got up and got to work.

In the cabin, I bent over the corpse and checked him—not to see if he was still breathing, not with a head shot like that. No, I wanted to see if the bullet had gone through and made a mess.

It hadn't. That was why so many people in my former profession used .22's—the bullet often didn't penetrate the far side of the skull, bouncing off bone and caroming around, making brain soup but keeping the mess inside the can.

Nothing to clean up in here. Like his young partner, this thoughtful prick also hadn't shit himself, so I was golden. Had he bled on that porous wood, there'd have been a stain even after clean-up. Better to be lucky than smart. Also better to be alive than dead.

But I still had to deal with getting rid of him and that kid on the fitness-center floor. The lake was frozen over, the gravel pits too, and there weren't enough critters around in the winter-time to chow down on the evidence. I would have to wrap them up and dump them somewhere. No way around it.

I walked back to the condo and got Janet's OxiClean laundry whitener, which also worked as a stain remover. I'd encouraged her to use that and not chlorine bleach, because OxiClean was known in my old trade as a DNA eater. I got a couple of old towels, too, and a roll of duct tape. And some rubber dish-washing gloves.

In the fitness center, the rubber gloves making it a little awk-ward, I rolled the dead kid over—typical ragged gaping exit wound in the back of his head—and cleaned up the gore with the towels. I found a plastic painter's tarp in the back room, rolled the kid up in it, secured him with duct tape, then dragged him past the pool and over to the front door.

I trotted across the highway to the lodge's rear parking lot and got in the kid's Impala and used his keys to start it. Soon I had backed it up to the front of the fitness center and loaded the plastic-wrapped body into the trunk. I won't lie to you. It winded me—a double bypass will do that to you, even if you swim every day.

Back in the condo, I got the fire going and burned the towels; the smell was nasty and it took a while. I packed a bag with several changes of clothes, three extra nine mil clips, and my toiletries. From my little safe I took several fake IDs, but had no current credit cards to go with them, so helped myself to five thousand in twenties and fifties. I locked up the condo and threw my bag in the back seat of the Impala, got in, and headed over to the cabin in the nearby woods.

Borrowing one of the sheets off the furniture, I mummy-wrapped the passive half of the team—really passive now—and duct-taped him up. Since he hadn't bled, finding plastic for him wasn't necessary, sheet would do fine. I dragged him out of there and across the little deck and down the steps, *clonk, clonk, clonk*, and he didn't feel a thing.

I threw the rest of his gear in the back seat, his suitcase and fridge and heater and so on, including the laptop. Somehow I got him stuffed in that trunk with the kid, but had to remove the spare and stow it in the back seat, too. I had a flashback to the time I'd done that in Biloxi, a long time ago. Made me smile.

But as I drove away from my condo and the Sylvan Lodge and the fitness center, its lights off now, I wasn't smiling. I was shaking my head, actually. All these years later and two bodies in the trunk again. Not exactly progress. Dawn was threatening the darkness and thoughts began bouncing around in my brain like that .22 slug in the backup guy's skull.

Had Susan Breedlove unwittingly led this pair here?

No. Those photos and the backup guy's surveillance set-up in the cabin made it a safe bet he'd been staking me out at least a week.

Could she have hired them? Or maybe be part of the hit team, sent in with a story to put me off balance while scoping out my digs?

No. She was for real—I'd read her book, and seen her author photo. That was the real her.

I'll be honest with you. When I took off in that Impala, I didn't have a plan. I was just driving this pair of stiffs and their shit away from where I lived and worked. To go somewhere and dump them that wasn't in my backyard.

Instinctively, however, I headed myself in the right direction even before I knew where I was going. I found myself on I-94, heading south.

Susan Breedlove lived in Davenport in the Quad Cities, where the Broker had done business—a coincidence that needed exploring, especially now that people had come looking to kill me. On top of that, Breedlove had been researching me for years now and might know something useful.

My eyes hurt from the glare of snow ricocheting off snow-banks—I'd left my sunglasses back in the Cadillac SUV. You can't think of everything. Tired and punchy, I checked into the Best Western Plus at Albert Lea, paying sixty-eight dollars cash for the privilege, no extra charge for the dead guys in the Impala trunk.

I slept damn near as soundly as they did, only in eight hours I was able to wake up.

And when I did, I knew exactly what I needed to do.

Most houses on River Drive, connecting Davenport and Betten-dorf (two of the Iowa/Illinois Quad Cities), might have been classified as mansions, and gothic ones at that, looming high and regal on the snowy bluff with a view of the Mississippi River with the nighttime lights of Rock Island across the way. A brick drive took me up to this outlier of a mid-twentieth century modern home, a low-slung pagoda affair, red-brick with count-less tall glass windows.

I guided my dreary gray Impala (mine now, since that dead kid didn't need it anymore) up a gently winding red-brick drive to where it widened to accommodate a two-car garage. I headed around the modernistic structure and up the walk, lined with snow-dusted shrubbery, the tall windows wearing a filigree of frost. I was in the military-style jacket, a long-sleeve burgundy t-shirt, black jeans and running shoes. The nine mil was in my right hand at my side. Bordering pines kept any nosy neighbors from noticing.

The .22 Browning Black Label 1911, wiped, had been left with the two wrapped corpses I'd deposited in a ditch on a lonely back road outside of Albert Lea. I'd been driving about four hours, with food and restroom stops, and, while not on top of my game, was alert enough to make this visit.

The red-brick walk, which took me under the roof's overhang, matched the brick of the house, and the many windows appeared to be more like walls. The front door was mostly glass, too. I rang the bell, only it turned out to be a buzzer, like when a contestant gets it wrong on a game show.

She responded right away, moving fluidly in loose white slacks and a black top that bared her shoulders, an outfit better suited for a girl in her twenties, but this woman in her forties carried it off just fine. Those big blue eyes and that stylishly mussed light-blonde hair stirred something in me, though not below the waist—she reminded me of someone, but I couldn't make the connection, a movie star maybe. Her mouth wasn't emblazoned red with lipstick this time, which made her look a little different but no less pretty. Her left hand was behind her back.

She looked at me through the glass, amused, interested, nothing more, as if viewing a creature safely in its cage.

"How did you find me?" she asked.

"You gave me your card," I said.

She laughed. "So I did."

We both had to keep our voices up—the glass was heavy, thick. No frost here though, enough heat in the house to prevent that, apparently.

She went on: "But you disappoint me. I figured you for

something dramatic. A midnight visit after breaking in. A fore-boding shape looming over my bed."

Writers.

I shrugged and showed her the nine mil, not in a threatening way. She laughed a little and displayed the baby Glock she had in her left hand.

"Could I come in?" I asked the glass.

"Certainly," she said.

She opened the door and cold air and I swept in. She shut the wood-framed glass slab behind me. There was no entryway to speak of—we were both immediately in a big open space, a roughly thirty-foot-square room with, just to my right, walls of glass providing a stunning view of the river at night with the city lights across the way making like Christmas, even though it wasn't Thanksgiving yet.

She made a gesture to take my coat and I shook my head. I nodded around the place. "Frank Lloyd Wright?"

"Good eye. No, a knock-off. Built the year you were born—you should feel at home."

The floor was gray concrete grooved like tile and the furniture, scattered tastefully around, was as mid-century modern as the house itself. What would have been nothing special when I was a kid was collector's item stuff now. Wood, fiberglass, metal. Straight lines, curved angles.

Her fireplace, a brick bulwark between glass walls, was bigger than mine and enthusiastically burning wood. Over it was a LeRoy Neiman painting of a platinum blonde Playboy Bunny, an incongruous decorative touch for a woman of the 2020s. Hell, they didn't even publish *Playboy* anymore. What was the world coming to?

That fireplace, which was crackling and snapping and summoning us with its warmth, dominated an area where on a throw rug of gold and gray geometric squares sat a modernistic yellow sofa, perfect for Captain Kirk and Lt. Uhura to lounge upon. Facing it was a slate gray coffee table with a David Hockney book on it, beyond which several squat beige arm-chairs dared us to see if their spindly wooden legs would hold up under the challenge.

Music was playing gently from somewhere—Peggy Lee singing "Black Coffee." That was Susan's cue.

"I'm having coffee," she said. "No hot chocolate in the house, I'm afraid. I can offer Coke Zero, if you like. Personally, I prefer it to Diet Coke."

"You have a refined palate. Uh, you have it in the can?"

"Yes."

"Don't open it."

"Why, d'you think I might drug you?"

"Or poison me. You met me at the door with a gun, after all."

"Good point." She rested her baby Glock on the slate gray coffee table. I put mine in a pocket of the military jacket, though I slipped out of the garment, folding it next to me, with that pocket handy.

I eyed the place while she was away. The few wall sections that weren't glass had framed abstract prints and an occasional painting. Recessed lighting created a sense of natural light.

None of this looked cheap, and these furnishings were either high-end reproductions or genuine collector's pieces. She had money, this girl. This woman. No sign of a man here, unless he had hung that Bunny picture. No, this was a female who had figured out how she liked to live.

Bobby Darin began singing, "You'd Be So Nice to Come To," softly.

She returned with her coffee in an angular coral-color cup and a can of Coke Zero for me. I popped the top, sipped, detected neither cyanide nor Mickey Finn, and set it on a coaster on the coffee table.

After settling in the chair across from me, she sat forward, her folded hands draped between her legs, and gave me a wicked little smile. "Second thoughts about that sequel?"

"Not exactly. I have a few questions."

"Please."

I kept my tone light. "I get that you have a general interest in true crime. But what got you interested in the subject matter of '*Sniper*' specifically?"

The fire used us as its dance floor for a flickering ballet. We were washed blue, then orange, then blue, then....

The smile got a little more wicked yet. "You mean interested in *you*?"

I raised a palm as if in court. "Let's not go there just yet. Why 'Quarry'?"

She sighed. Retrieved her coffee cup from the coaster where she'd deposited it. Sipped. Sat back, holding onto the cup.

"Actually, you have it backward," she said.

"How so?"

"It was…'Quarry'…that got me interested in true crime. There were killings in the QC area…the killings you wrote about in your first 'novel'…that made it into the papers around here. Articles in the Quad City *Times*, the Rock Island *Argus*. About these real local crimes that had been 'fictionalized.'"

"I wasn't aware of that," I admitted.

"Not that it was a big deal or anything," she said with a shrug. "Just a few stories in the papers at the time."

"Wouldn't that have been *before* your time?"

She nodded. "But a reporter on the *Times* named Lehman collected a bunch of his columns in *Notorious Quad Cities*, a locally published book that included write-ups on the real crimes echoed in the sleazy '*Quarry*' paperbacks."

I didn't see what was "sleazy" about it, though I let that pass.

She was saying, "Enter an impressionable young woman not long out of college...a journalism major? And the rest is history —*your* history."

"But you didn't write about that right away. Those other books came first, that one about the Unabomber, another on Casey Anthony."

"Right. And a couple others, 'ripped from the headlines.' Along the way I gathered information about Quarry...should I call you that, Jack? Quarry?"

"Jack is fine."

Nina Simone started in on "Feelin' Good."

"Anyway," Susan said, "as I built my reputation, and my books made the bestseller lists, that pet story of mine became saleable, and PTSD became fashionable."

"I was always ahead of my time," I said.

"I've lived in this area all my life," she said with a toss of all that blonde hair. "What can I say? The local connection drew me to the material."

"The material," I said. "My life, you mean."

She sat forward again, the coffee cup in her hands as if warming them, though the fire made that unnecessary. "So, if you haven't had second thoughts about that sequel, what brings you here, Jack? Not to *kill* me, I hope."

That was an option I hadn't completely ruled out.

But I said, "Of course not."

"So? Why *are* you here?"

I told her that a hit team had been sent to kill me, since she and I had last talked, and that I'd handled it, though that still left me marked for murder. Her expression grew grave in the telling.

" 'Marked for murder,' " she said, and shivered. She looked pale now, even in the glow of the fire. "It sounds so...melodramatic."

"Not when you're the one marked for it," I said.

She frowned at me in thought. "*How* did you deal with them?"

"Do you really want to know?"

"I do."

"Off the record?"

She nodded.

I told her, briefly. Not in detail. Or anyway not in great detail.

When I was finished, she said, with not a drop of blood in her face, "And they were in your trunk while you slept in some motel?"

"It was a Best Western."

"And you left them in a ditch in the boonies somewhere, on your way here?"

"That's what I said."

Sammy Davis began singing "What Kind of Fool Am I?"

She was staring past me, perhaps out the frost-patched window/wall over my shoulder.

I asked, "Is it getting through to you yet?"

"…what?"

"That this isn't abstract. That this isn't 'melodrama.' It's life and death, and in this case it's my life and death, and I take that goddamn fucking serious."

She swallowed, her eyebrows flicking up and back down. "I don't blame you. Are you…wondering if I led them to you? I didn't! I swear I didn't!"

The big blue eyes were even bigger now. Finally she was afraid. Good.

"I know you didn't lead them to me," I said.

"You…trust me, then?"

"Oh hell no. But the timing isn't right for you to lead them to me. Look, I'm long retired. I haven't done anything in the last decade and a half that would make anybody want me dead. I'm a pussycat in my old age."

"I noticed," she said.

"But you've been researching me—me and my life, me and who I used to be."

"You're admitting it. You're Quarry."

"Of course I'm fucking Quarry! Will you help me?"

"And if I don't," she said softly, "I'll be in the next ditch?"

"No," I said.

Maybe.

She swallowed thickly. "I'm already a danger to you, aren't I?"

"Can you be of help to me?"

Her answer was a question: "You didn't find anything out from those two…killers, did you?"

"No. One I dealt with straightaway, and the other I questioned first, but all I got out of him was that his jobs came over the Net."

She grunted. "I wish I had access to his computer."

I shrugged. "I've got his laptop in the car."

That surprised her. I'd mentioned that I thrown a bunch of the backup guy's shit out in that ditch, just getting rid of it. That I stomped on and pitched the cell phone with the pics of me and my place. But I'd held onto the laptop, figuring it might be useful.

"They are almost certainly from the Midwest," I said, "unless things have radically changed since my day."

"How so?"

"Well, this is something you didn't quite figure, at least not in the book you published. The 'brokers' in the contract killing business, at least in my day, worked a region or anyway an area. That's why almost all of my jobs were in the Midwest."

"I noticed that."

"So it's a reasonable assumption the middleman this team worked through is in the Midwest. I might be full of shit on this, in this computer age. But for a long time there was a regional slant to this business."

"Okay."

I leaned forward. "You've been digging into my past. Can you think of any possible red flags? Anybody with a reason, after all this time, to send somebody to take me out?"

She thought about that for what seemed a long time. Then, very slowly, she nodded. "I can. There's one possibility in Memphis. Another in Biloxi. And, yes, one right here in the Quad Cities."

"I could see why certain parties in Memphis and Biloxi might have issues with me. And the Quad Cities…would that be something to do with the Broker?"

She nodded. "Yes. I was living in Port City with my mother when that *Notorious Quad Cities* book came out. It said that this Broker of yours had mob connections, despite his sterling reputation in the QC's. I went to the library and looked up the original coverage in the local papers."

I was squinting at her, trying to bring her into focus. "Port City? You lived in Port City?"

That had been the little town nearby where I'd done the job that led to the conflict between Broker and me—which had led to the death of one of us.

"Yes, with my mother," she said. "Margaret Baker. Peg Baker. She had a restaurant/bar I helped her with for a while, summers while I was in college, and a while after that. She was kind of a local celebrity—she was in *Playboy* magazine, in a 'Bunnies of Chicago' spread. That's her."

She pointed to the painting over the fireplace. Then she just sat there staring at me, waiting for a reaction.

I gave her one: "What is that, your married name? Susan Breedlove?"

"Yes."

"Where's your husband?"

"I divorced him. He ran around and stole money from me. Thank God we didn't have any kids." She shuddered. "I should've hired you to kill him."

"What's your maiden name?"

"Baker, of course."

No wonder she looked so familiar to me.

"Listen," I said. "There's something else I need to ask you."

"Sure."

"Are you…are you my daughter?"

Her laugh was just a little shrill. "You *are* slipping, aren't you, Quarry? Just figuring that out now, are you? Shall we get swabbed and send for one of those DNA tests or is what my mother told me about you enough?"

SEVEN

My daughter put me up for the night, saving her old man the cost of a room, which was darn generous of her, considering I hadn't done much for her in the four decades plus of her lifetime, other than bang her mother and go on about my business.

The guest room, one of three bedrooms down a narrow hall (one had been converted to an office), wasn't spacious; but the bed was comfy and the glass walls had blackout curtains. The few sections of wall that weren't glass had photos of various Frank Lloyd Wright homes and buildings and the nightstand bore a coffee-table book full of pictures and information on the architect. Considering whoever erected this place had ripped the old boy off, that seemed either gracious or shameless.

Anyway, I slept like a stone. The revelation about my fatherhood might well have made a wakeful, restless mess out of me. But after a day of driving and corpse disposal, I couldn't have gone under faster if anesthetized.

I got out of bed, having slept in my sweats. I was gathering my toiletries bag at a dresser when she stuck her head in. Her hair was ponytailed back and she wore no makeup; she was in a white terry robe and looked about twenty.

"Good," she said, "you're up. Shower is yours. Breakfast in half an hour."

She disappeared.

The bathroom was that same red brick with wood trim and had a tub with a showerhead and curtain. The fixtures were light green and vintage. The space was surprisingly small but I managed to shower and scrape beard off my face and brush my teeth without bruising myself. Even worked taking a dump into the program. You'd rather have a sex scene or a shootout, but I don't make it with my own offspring, nor do I turn her house into the OK Corral unless absolutely necessary.

In a fresh long-sleeve dark green t-shirt, black jeans and running shoes, I lumbered up the hall and through the Great Room (as Janet would have called it) and into the kitchen. It was small, too—cypress wood everywhere, cabinets and counters and even the scaled-down picnic-style table. No wall-to-ceiling glass here, just a normal window and a larger one onto the big living room. The appliances were up to date, though compact versions. Susan was at the stove scrambling eggs. Sausage links were frying. Thank God. What if I'd spawned a vegetarian?

She'd made biscuits, too. I was hungry and it all tasted good. She provided me with orange juice while she had coffee and, as we sat across from each other, little was said. I could tell she was mulling something, but not yet ready to talk. I helped her clear the table and wiped it down with a wet rag, then we sat again. She brought along more coffee for herself and a Coke Zero for me.

I thanked her, sipped it, then asked her, "Get anything out of that laptop?"

"Had to get past the password first. Didn't have a birthday or anniversary to try. Went with all the predictable ones, 123456, qwerty, even 'password.' Finally figured it."

"What was it?"

"Quarry—all caps."

I took that in, then said, "They seemed to know who they were after."

She nodded. "And I think I know what our next step is."

"Our?"

"We have a road trip ahead and you're going to need me for more than driving."

"Am I?"

She got a little cocky now, which added to how young she seemed, unless you really looked at her. "That laptop proved very helpful. Wasn't hard at all to go through the e-mails and figure out which ones were coded messages to your two midnight callers."

It was more like three A.M. callers, but I couldn't see correcting her.

I asked, "How hard was it to crack? You must have what the kids call 'mad skills.' "

She shook her head. "No I don't, not in this case anyway. I overstated it, saying 'coded.' Basically it's just e-mails that stay purposely vague—inquiring about availability for a job but no specifics."

"Then how did they communicate?"

"Well, that much is spelled out. It doesn't take a Navajo code breaker to figure out a requested 'burner convo' is a conversation using burner phones. The e-mails include the number to call and when to do so. Always a different number."

"What does that give us?"

She had me doing it now: *us*.

"Hitting you," she said, "seems to have been set up about a month ago. Again, there's no real specifics, except the burner phone numbers on the e-mailer's end…and that doesn't give us anything, obviously, because each one is used only once, the phone pitched." She shrugged, sipped coffee. "But that's irrelevant."

"Why?"

"I already know who sent the e-mail and where they were sending it from. I even know the address."

"The 'IP' address? What, are you some kind of hacker, too?"

She laughed. Got up and poured herself some more coffee at the cypress counter, saying as she did, "No! The street address. Business address, also. I don't know jack about computers. Oh, I know more than *you* do, but...anyway, I recognized the e-mail address."

"Why would you be able to do that?"

Sun from the side window came in over the kitchen counter making her light-blonde hair even lighter; she looked like Peg Baker, all right.

"Because," she said, "I had e-mail correspondence with this particular party when I was researching the new book. I spoke with him on the phone several times and did an in-person, on-site interview last month."

This is where, in the movies, they say, *Holy shit!* Well, one of the places.

"Who is 'this particular party'?" I asked.

She was back with her fresh cup. "His name is Wesley Culver. He owns and operates Culver Gallery, an antiques shop in Minneapolis. His partner, for many years, was the woman you called 'Lu' in two of your books. I interviewed him about her and he claims to know nothing about the possibility that she'd once been active in your onetime profession...or that later she became a rare female 'broker,' as you would put it, for contract killers."

"You didn't ever talk to Lu herself?"

"No. She died before I began the project."

"...Died."

Susan winced. "Yes. I'm sorry. For some reason, I figured you'd know. That was thoughtless of me....She was shot and killed at the gallery, taking an after-hours appointment with an antiques dealer from Colorado, who the police now say never existed. Obviously it could have had something to do with her activities in the murder-for-hire business. But it also could have been a robbery that had been put in motion under false pretenses by a phony buyer—some valuable pieces were missing, Culver says. The police report said the antiques shop in Denver was real enough, but the 'dealer' presenting himself as their rep wasn't....Are you all right?"

Lu was someone who'd walked into my life twice, with a considerable number of years between encounters, though for a while after that second time we had stayed in touch. Not as coworkers or, when she was taking on a Broker-like role, business associates. Friends. We'd taken several vacations together. Normal human being stuff. We each had secrets we didn't have to keep from each other, and that was nice. I had kind of loved her, and she had sort of loved me.

No, I didn't tear up. Fuck you! I just felt empty. Hollow. The Broker, by which I mean *the* Broker, had early on given me the cute code name Quarry because he said I was hard and hollow inside, like a played-out rock quarry. I felt hollow, all right, but not so hard.

"Jack...I said, are you all right?"

"Yes. Yes. It's just...when you hear someone you know has died, but haven't seen them for some time...when they haven't been in your life much at all lately...it's tough to..."

"Process?"

I shrugged. "As good a word as any. But this guy Culver. The messages to my two callers the other night—those were from his regular e-mail address?"

She nodded. "The same one he used with me and I presume for all his e-correspondence."

"Not much security sense."

She returned my shrug, barely used. "Well, he's an old guy. Not exactly a computer whiz."

"*How* old?"

She flipped a hand. "Oh, his fifties, easily."

"He *does* sound over the fuckin' hill."

Her grin was her mother's. "I thought that would get a rise out of you. So. Minneapolis is maybe five hours away as we sit here. Should I call Culver and make an appointment?"

"No. Sometimes a cold call is just the thing."

"Like when I dropped by your place."

"Yeah. And like when I dropped by this place."

"So. Road trip?"

I nodded. "Road trip."

We took Susan's car, a Cadillac CT5, silver. The Impala was something of a beater, plus I didn't have papers on it. And it hadn't been thoroughly gone over to cleanse it of blood and other trace evidence that might make the forensics girls and boys giddy.

We'd just got onto I-35 when I said, "I have a Cadillac. Same color as this."

Satellite radio was playing an easy listening station—Johnny Mathis, "Chances Are." She seemed to like her mother's era better than her own.

"I know you do," she said. The ponytail was gone, the blonde hair fluffy and touching her shoulders. "I saw it at your place. An SUV."

"You don't have to smirk when you say it."

She was in a turtleneck sweater with wide stripes of cream, black, brown, and yellow with matching suede boots, and her brown skirt was almost a mini—I wasn't sure I approved.

"Sorry," she said, still smirking. "It's just—you can afford a Cadillac, and you choose an SUV? You *are* old."

"It's a fact," I admitted. "Are you rich, kid?"

"Enough."

"From writing?"

A little shrug. "Well, I sell a lot of books. Four TV miniseries.

Options for a couple more that haven't got made. It adds up. That sequel starting to sound good to you?"

"You could've cut me in on the *Sniper* one, you know."

"Why, did you like it?"

"Not particularly. But I would've cashed the check."

"You *are* a writer at heart."

I drove after a while. She'd been up late, poking around in that laptop, so she napped a bit. When we crossed into Minnesota, she took over. I don't know Minneapolis that well.

"You want to hear about my mother?" she asked.

I hadn't asked. Didn't want to intrude.

"If you like," I said.

"She never married. She lived with a few guys, but she had a thing for this young Vietnam vet she met in '75. The one who knocked her up. She never told me, till your first book came out, about who she thought you were."

"She figured out I killed people."

Susan nodded. "She did. Yet she said you were very nice."

"That's me all over. Was she happy?"

"Happy enough. Her bar and restaurant business stayed profitable for a long, long time. She was about my age when she died. Breast cancer. Ironic, huh? Famous for posing topless, and her tits kill her."

I said, "That's not ironic."

"It isn't?"

"No. You need to learn the difference between irony and tragedy."

We didn't talk for a while after that.

While we sat in a booth eating an unhealthy truck stop meal, she looked up at me with a smile that wasn't convincing and asked, "You aren't sitting there trying to figure out whether you should kill your daughter or not, are you? That's a real Quarry-type conundrum."

An old woman in the adjacent table turned to Susan quickly, startled, then turned away as the codger across from her shook his head and raised a hand in a "none of your business" way. I say "old woman" and "codger," but they were probably not that much older than me.

I said, "Would have been fun raising you."

"Spare the rod?"

That got a smile out of me. "You have any kids?"

"No. Don't worry. You're not a grandfather."

"You don't seem to mind, not having any."

She made a face. "Would've just tied me more to that prick I stupidly married. No questions about that, please. Anyway, can't have any. Kids. Something wrong inside me."

Something was wrong inside a lot of us.

In a Southwest Minneapolis neighborhood called Fulton, at the busy intersection of 50th and Xerxes, antiques shops and home stores dominated. On a weekend an area like this would be swarming with shoppers, but it was cold and lightly snowing on this mid-afternoon on a weekday and business was as dead as two bodies in a ditch.

Just north a few blocks on its own half a block squatted a big three-story '40s-era cream-brick building with black shutters on its white-trimmed windows and a big bold black-and-white sign on a one-story matching annex saying

CULVER GALLERY
art, antiques and
quality household goods

with days, times of business, phone number, and website below.

Susan left her immodest ride in the modest parking lot and led me inside into a world of large ornate, formal furniture from previous centuries. The walls were populated with oil paintings, mostly portraits of ancestors who seemed disappointed in us, and on our either side were roll-top desks, Tiffany lamp shades, and dining room sets that had been pricey in their day and were out of the question in ours. The heat was working overtime and we slipped out of our wintry jackets and slung them over an arm.

The place smelled like furniture polish, which was better than dust, and several professional-looking middle-aged women in conservative dresses and beauty-shop hair smiled and nodded at us as we moved through the lavish array of vintage goods. From the easily visible price tags, the place didn't seem anxious to move anything. Maybe it was one of those businesses that could make it on a few big-ticket items a week. But I already had an idea that what kept this gallery afloat had nothing to do with antiques.

In back was a long mahogany-and-glass counter filled with costume jewelry and collectibles, with the register over at right. I'd been wondering why the counter wasn't up front, but they were positioned near the back room with its overflow merchandise and double garage doors for furniture to be loaded up and out.

The counter was empty while we stood there for maybe thirty seconds, then one of the little army of middle-aged gals got in back of it to see if she could help. Getting a better look at Susan, the woman beamed and said, "Why, Ms. Breedlove! What an unexpected pleasure. Are you shopping with us today? Or perhaps you're researching some new old Minneapolis crimes?"

Susan gave the friendly woman a warm smile. "Nice to see you again, Nancy. I'm hoping for a follow-up interview with Mr. Culver. Is he in?"

Nancy seemed genuinely disappointed that she had to disappoint. "Oh, I'm afraid not. Mr. Culver's semi-retired now, you know. He only comes in three days a week, afternoons, and this isn't one of them. He'll be here tomorrow, though."

Susan cocked her head, mildly let down. "Well, I should have called. I was in town visiting relatives…this is my father, by the way."

"How do you do, Mr. Breedlove," Nancy said, and offered a gentle hand across the counter, which I took and shook. "Are you a local?"

"No, in for a family reunion," I said. "Lot of breeding and loving went on in this neck of the woods."

That got a nervous laugh from Nancy and a curdled smile from Susan.

"You might catch Mr. Culver at home," Nancy said. "I'm sure he wouldn't mind. I could call ahead…?"

"No, no," Susan said, waving it off. "What time's he in tomorrow?"

"Around one. Right after lunch."

"I'll catch him then."

We slipped back into our jackets and exited through the well-polished private property of dead people, then stepped outside into colder air than even Iowa could summon. At least the snow had stopped.

Shivering a little, Susan said, "You aren't as funny as you think you are."

"I'm pretty funny. Why are we waiting till tomorrow to see Culver?"

"We aren't."

"You're a take-charge girl, aren't you?"

"Do you know where Culver lives?"

"No."

"Then I better be."

❖

The cream-and-brown Tudor—with its pitched roof, overlapping gables and half-timbering—was one of a row of pricey '20s-era residences on West Dean Parkway that had both a homey and historic feel, all sitting up top of the same snowy slope with perfectly shoveled walks from the street to their well-set-back front doors.

Across the way were lush woods beyond which was Bde Maka Ska, Lake Calhoun having recently been restored to its Native American name. Opposite the house in question, luck had provided a snow-and-gravel turn-around between street and sidewalk that the Cadillac could be pulled up and into. And this was the kind of neighborhood where a stray Caddy or two would hardly be noticed.

We made the trek up the slope and its steps, some icy snow flecking us, blowing not snowing. We'd had a meal over which we'd discussed our strategy, and it was now early evening. Lights burned yellow in this and the neighboring houses, indicating more life than the sparse traffic and the empty sidewalks implied.

Susan pressed the bell and chimes came from within. The massive dark-brown door, which matched the decorative timbering, had a small window and, shortly, eyes peered through at us.

Then the door opened and a thin man who had apparently purchased a mustache from the Clark Gable estate regarded us with big dark eyes, narrow mouth, and cleft chin in a sunken-cheeked face. His suspiciously black hair was cut short. He wore a long-sleeved white shirt and a black-and-white tie, his slacks black.

The narrow mouth formed an uneasy smile. "Ms. Breedlove. What a nice surprise." The uninflected baritone didn't convey that sentiment.

"I'm so sorry just to drop by," she said, a hair shy of obsequious. "My father and I were in town for a family reunion…" We'd decided to hold onto that lie, in case we needed it. "…and I wanted to say hello."

"Hello," he said with a smile. He had gotten his Adam's apple from the Don Knotts estate, it would seem.

We were still on the stoop in the cold, by the way.

"And, frankly," she said, feigning embarrassment, "I have a few follow-up questions after our interview last month, and wondered if you could put up with me…with us…for a few minutes."

He bowed his head, said, "Certainly," and gestured us in like a horror host to a TV-set crypt.

But there was nothing crypt-like about the interior—the vintage woodwork and everything historic about the place had been blotted out by white in a way that would have left this antiques dealer aghast if confronted with a 1900s dresser whose finish had been so demeaned.

The effect, the desired one I would imagine, was to make the old house modern, and made a suitable setting for the very modern furniture and block-color abstract art sparsely spotted around for dabs of red and black and blue. Nothing antique here—he must have gotten sick of that at the gallery.

He collected our jackets and put them in a closet under the white front stairs under the white ceiling—at least the new-looking wood flooring was brown. Then he ushered us off to the left where a living room was furnished in a way that made Susan's mid-century modern pieces look ancient. A bright blue sofa popped at right and a gray two-seater lurked in a corner, with a brown leather-and-wood bench dividing the room vertically, and a gas fireplace with no hearth going, cut out of a rectangular slab of wood designed to break up all that goddamn white.

Culver sat himself on the bench facing us on the blue couch, where he'd deposited us. A long, low-slung white coffee table with nothing on it stretched horizontally before us. He had his hands folded in his lap and hunched forward slightly.

"I am going to be a terrible host," he said, as if he were proud of it. "I'm afraid I have a prior engagement, and only have a few minutes for you. I have a client to see, a private showing at the gallery."

"Well, that reminds me," Susan said, "of the specific question I had for you."

Eyebrows climbing a high forehead. "Oh?"

She got her phone out of her purse and began to record.

"Your late partner, Louise Benson," she said. That was the name Lu had been using here. "I've been exploring that meeting she had that turned so tragic."

"Terrible," he said and shuddered. "She was a lovely woman. Incredible business mind, and a good eye for finds at estate sales. Much missed."

"Yes, you'd said that earlier. But this antiques business in Colorado—had you done business with them before?"

"I had."

"With the specific person Louise was meeting with?"

"No. He presented himself to her as a new employee of that firm. When the police looked into it, he did not exist. The real dealers knew nothing of him."

"Thanks for confirming that. Your inventory showed some pieces missing?"

"Yes, some high-ticket items. This was very likely a robbery gone awry."

I knew she was going over old ground. We weren't really after anything specific—this visit was to give me a chance to size up the guy. Was he the new Broker?

Susan said, "Well, since we last spoke, I've confirmed beyond doubt Louise's criminal activities. Were you at all suspicious that she might be conducting what turned out to be a murder-for-hire business from the gallery?"

He bristled. "Ms. Breedlove, I've said from the beginning that this sordid side of Louise Benson's activities came as a complete and utter surprise to me. That none of these criminal associates ever darkened the gallery's door. I thought I'd made that clear in our previous conversation."

Footsteps coming down the stairs in the outer area caught my attention. Susan's, too.

A man about forty with well-carved features leaned in at the archway entry to the living room. Six foot or so, he was blond and tan and his muscular build was not hidden by his yellow sweater and peach trousers, and he looked like an aging surfer who'd lost his way. "Sorry to butt in....Wes, are you sure you don't need me tonight?"

"I'll be fine," he said. "You'd be bored to tears, Vic, it's that *wretched* woman from *Kenwood*....oh, Ms. Breedlove, Mr. Breedlove, this is my husband, Vic."

We nodded and smiled and Vic nodded and smiled.

Vic got his coat from the closet, a faux-fur hooded bomber jacket, climbed into it, tossed a wave and went out.

I asked our host, "So, then, you're his wife?"

Culver bristled. "I'm *his* husband. We're each other's husband."

His eyes were hard and cold now.

"I just didn't know how it worked," I said, and gave him an embarrassed smile and shrug.

"Apparently not." He turned those chilly eyes on Susan. "Is there anything else?"

She said no and we got to our feet, as did our host, and as we headed for the door, Susan said, "I am really sorry to have stopped by out of the blue, and I don't mean to impose. But I may need to talk to you again, if you're willing."

He warmed up, to her at least. "Of course. Just give me a little notice next time."

As we walked down the many steps to the street, Susan said, "Are you some kind of homophobe?"

"I was working with a gay partner," I said, "when you were just a twinkle in my eye. I was just getting a bead on the guy."

In the car, still parked there but with the motor going, Susan said, "It's hard for me to see Wesley Culver as a likely candidate for a 'broker' who took over for your Lu."

"I have no trouble doing that. And I think he probably arranged her murder so he could take over."

"Oh, come on, Jack. He's not the type!"

"Are *you* some kind of homophobe? That house is worth a couple million. He's got a gallery full of stuff that nobody wants to buy, particularly at those prices. It's a front and it's a money laundry. That 'husband' is as much a bodyguard as a boy toy—he had a gun in a jacket pocket."

"Maybe he was just glad to see you."

That made me laugh, and she laughed, too. It would suck to have a kid without a sense of humor.

She said, "My research says Culver is civic-minded—very active in charity work and support of the arts, and he's been a respected antiques dealer for almost three decades."

"Maybe," I said, "but he's got shark eyes."

"What do you suggest?"

"Let's follow him to that meeting, and when it's over, *I'll* conduct the next interview. He can talk into my nine millimeter."

EIGHT

I was at the wheel now, with Susan navigating. An access alley —well, more a paved drive—was behind the row of mostly Tudor houses on West Dean Parkway. We were parked at the curb just down and across from the alley's mouth, waiting for Culver, to see if he really was meeting a client.

"Something about that didn't ring true," I told her. "I doubt he's meeting a client at the gallery."

She looked at me curiously. "Maybe it's something to do with his *other* business."

"No, we know he conducts *that* mostly online. I think he was just getting rid of us."

"Then why lie to Vic about it?"

"Just a hunch. If he hasn't left the house within an hour, we're dropping in again. Through the door, unannounced."

But I was wrong—he did have an appointment, or anyway he left the house in a BMW sedan right after I predicted he wouldn't. The vehicle was white with black accents, of course. Yes, this boy had money.

Though it had been a while, I had plenty of experience with tailing somebody. Back in the day, the Broker insisted the active half of a hit team needed to trade off occasionally with the passive half, so each was familiar and comfortable in either role. After all, a passive specialist needed to be able to handle himself when the active side required backup.

And when I'd been working the Broker's list to find clients, I would have to stake out the name I'd selected from that list for extended surveillance, to see where he was headed, and determine who the target was. Sometimes that work lasted a month or more. So a shadow job was old hat to me.

On the other hand, traffic was fairly light, meaning I had to stay two or even three cars behind Culver to keep from being made. His wheels were distinctive, though, which helped, and the route didn't take many twists and turns.

We crossed West Lake Street then headed south on the former Calhoun Parkway with a lake view at our left and tree-nestled affluence on our right. He went along at a good clip but never broke the speed limit more than a mile or two. Before long the residential area was clearly an income tier down from before but still nothing to sneeze at. Then it seemed I'd been proven wrong a second time.

We were on Xerxes Avenue South.

"He's heading for the gallery," Susan said.

"Maybe," I said, but she was probably right. Our route, which had required crossing any number of major thoroughfares, made more sense now.

We were in an area Susan said was called Linden Hills—families and young professionals lived here, close to bars, restaurants, coffee shops, parks. And that included the hub of antiquing off of which the Culver Gallery resided. But then the black-trimmed white BMW rolled right by the entrance to the gallery's little parking lot.

So I hadn't been wrong…though had no idea yet why.

As we kept going, the residential aspect dropped a notch and then we were in a world of liquor stores, auto parts, and laundromats. Finally Culver slowed and pulled in at a big plastic sign with blue sky over dark blue waves, superimposed with

LAKE CITY

M O T E L

on a brick pedestal. The whole motel was brick, tan and black and brown—a typical one-story row of rooms, probably the nicest motel Bonnie and Clyde ever stayed at.

Right across the street was the Lyndale Avenue Baptist Church, where we pulled into the parking lot.

"*This*," I told her, "is irony."

I shut off the engine and we watched. Culver drove past the free-standing check-in building and pulled in all the way down in front of Number Twelve—a Harley was parked up on the sidewalk between Twelve and Eleven, which had nothing in its vehicle slot. Only two other rooms had cars in their spaces and that was way at the other end. Slow night for adultery.

Speaking of which, when Culver knocked on the door of Twelve, a six-footer with a burr haircut, shovel jaw and close-set tiny eyes answered immediately. Maybe twenty-five, this guy was truth in advertising: his black t-shirt said

ROUGH TRADE
ATHLETIC DEPT

over white boxer briefs. No tattoos obvious, lending a touch of class. Culver went in and the burr-haircut biker shut them inside.

"I hate it," I said, "when husbands cheat on husbands. Where's their moral compass?"

"Pointing north, probably," she said.

We watched, not sure what to do. Susan pointed out the church's announcement sign, which said

CHURCH PARKING
TRESPASSERS
WILL BE BAPTIZED

and asked if that was irony, too. I said it wasn't. That was farce.

"Why don't we book a room," she said.

I gave her a look.

"Not *here!*" she said. "Someplace nicer."

"Like a Motel 6? No, we're in for the long haul. Culver's got to go home in time to be there when his hubby returns. We'll follow him back and you will knock again. He'll answer. You apologize and ask another round of irritating questions and then excuse yourself to use the bathroom. That other door under the stairs by the coat closet is probably a john. That allows you to go over and let me in the front door, then you slip out and wait in the car...but park it by the mouth of the alley."

"Why will I be waiting in the car?"

So she wouldn't see me doing what I might have to do to get information out of the owner of the Culver Gallery.

"So you can hit the horn twice if overage surfer boy Vic shows up before I'm done."

"If he does, what will you do?"

"Improvise."

Another car pulled in at the Lake City Motel, a sporty-looking late-model Audi, metallic red. It didn't stop at the check-in shack, either, but rolled over cautiously toward the black-trimmed white BMW and pulled into the open space outside Eleven.

I glanced at Susan and she glanced at me.

The surfer dude hubby got out of the Audi and walked over to the Harley on the sidewalk between Eleven and Twelve and for a moment stood regarding it with contempt. Then he strode, almost ran, over to the door of Twelve and pounded three times with the blunt edge of a fist.

Susan glanced at me and I glanced at her.

The door to Twelve cracked open, Surfer Vic pushed his way through and the door closed. Slammed, really—we heard it in the church parking lot.

Nothing for maybe thirty seconds.

Then the door burst open and the surfer tossed the biker out onto the sidewalk in a pile, the latter's face bloodied and the former's face an angry mask, almost as red as the bloodied one. Then came a black leather jacket with lots of metal which, on his hands and knees, the biker grabbed before scrambling for the Harley and getting on, starting the engine up, while the surfer shook a blood-smeared fist and yelled, *"Go! Get the fuck out! Just get the fuck out!"*

We heard that in the church lot, too.

Then a woebegone Culver appeared in the doorway of Twelve, with his shirt unbuttoned and his pants off, briefs too. His feet were bare, but that dangling lengthy dick was the attention grabber. He was crying but also angry. The two stood in front of the motel room raging at each other, breaths smoking in the cold, the surfer towering over the older man and apparently on the edge of exploding into further violence.

But then the younger man sucked the anger in and shoved Culver away and went back to the Audi as quickly as he'd come and got back into the vehicle, firing it up. Like a demented car hop, the barefoot, dick-dangling Culver went around to the driver's window and yelled at it plaintively, the argument in him turning to something pitiful. Cold had shrunk his dick, adding further indignity.

None of this yelling, screaming, and pleading had made itself specifically heard, only the occasional thundercrack word emerging from the storm of fury.

Now Culver padded back pathetically toward the room and I got out of the Caddy with hand in the military jacket pocket and around the nine mil. I leaned back in.

"Stay here," I said.

Her eyes were huge. *"What?"*

"You heard me. Get behind the wheel. Crawl over. Better stay down. We may be leaving quickly."

"Jack! *Quarry!*"

I paused for a few moments before crossing, waiting till the street was empty of traffic, and then all that swimming paid off, because the running came easy. I was across the narrow parking lot and on the gallery owner before the door could close. I shouldered my way in, taking him with me, shutting the door behind me hard. He tumbled and skidded face down on a carpet that you really wouldn't want to get that close to.

The cramped little room had it all—piss-yellow pebbled walls, paint-peeling ceiling, low-wattage nightstand lamp with a crooked scorched shade, beat-up cheap dresser with a cracked mirror, the smell of stale cigarette smoke, and so much more.

"Put your pants on," I commanded, the nine mil in my hand indicating the scarred-up chair that some of his things were folded on. He swallowed, got to his feet, and started with his boxer briefs—black with DOLCE & GABBANA boldly white on the band—then his trousers.

"The socks can wait," I said. "Sit."

I directed him to the foot of the bed, where he sat on the edge. He was light but the mattress lowered nearly to the floor. That just goes to show that a man can fuck on anything. His black hair, though short, was mussed and the shark eyes were hooded with the whites red-streaked; his mustache looked wilted and his head hung.

"What is this about?" he asked. It was like a Highway Patrolman stopped him when he wasn't speeding.

I was facing this dejected creature with the dresser to my back and the door in easy view. "You took over for Lu, didn't you?"

The eyes un-hooded and he frowned. "Who *are* you? Not Susan Breedlove's father!"

Actually, I was, but I didn't correct him.

"I'm Quarry," I said. "Does that name mean anything to you?"

But I already knew the answer, because all the blood had drained from his already pale face.

"Should it?" he asked.

I trained the nine mil on him. "Shouldn't it?"

His raised his hands a little, palms out, in surrender. "I worked with Lu a long time and then, after somebody killed her, I stepped in. Is that what you want to know?"

My grin must have been an awful thing. "First of all, if you didn't have her killed, to take over the business, I am very damn surprised."

"No! I would never do that! We worked together for years! What kind of person do you think I am?"

"The kind who has been the middleman between clients and contract killers. A broker. The broker in this Midwestern region who sent two assholes to kill me, and if you're wondering why you haven't heard from them yet, they're two dead assholes now."

The surrender hands came up again. "I admit I took over Lu's business. But I didn't have her killed, and I didn't carry a contract on you. I don't know a goddamn thing about this! But maybe I can send you in the right direction. There's no need for violence."

I swung the nine millimeter and the side of the barrel hit him across his left cheek opening a diagonal cut that dripped red like a sloppy paint job. He yowled and with my free hand I tossed him a box of Kleenex from the nightstand. He held some tissues to the cheek. He was crying.

"I swear I know nothing of this. Jesus, Quarry—you must know there are a dozen brokers working the trade in this country. This wasn't me! Why do you think it is?"

"Because, dumbass, you used your own e-mail address to communicate with that kid and his bald backup. Then baldie took his laptop on the job with him. I'm glad I got out of this business before the idiots took over."

He replaced the bloody tissues with some fresh ones and his crying turned into sobs. "Please don't kill me. Please don't kill me."

Like I would leave this prick alive.

"I have no intention of killing you," I said, "unless you don't level with me. Want to take a run at it?"

He started to nod, swallowed, snuffled snot, swallowed some more, and said, "It was my contract, okay, it was, but things are different now."

"Different how?"

"This came through multiple intermediaries. That's standard these days. My contact with them is strictly over the Net. Money by way of wire transfers. Burner-phone conversations. This is insulated like you wouldn't believe."

Actually, I did believe.

"Then I need you to share all of it with me," I said. "Every e-mail address, all bank information, any phone number that isn't a burner."

The eyes swam with hysteria now. "I can't do that here!"

"Well, you can put your socks on and we can go home, and you can do it there."

The door burst open, kicked hard.

It was the Rough Trade biker in the black leather jacket, like he was late for the Village People audition, only he was armed —that was a silenced .22 Ruger unless I missed my bet.

And he didn't miss his: the gun coughed and the bullet traveled through Culver's left temple and across through the open door of a bathroom made even filthier by the spray of blood, bone and brains, some of which glopped onto the mirror and began a smeary slide.

Here's the bad part about automatics: they can jam on you.

And did Rough Trade's automatic jam on him, saving my ass?

No. My automatic jammed on me and I was looking right into that silenced .22's staring-back eye and I swear my thought was, *Well, it took long enough to get here.*

But then a noise—like a single scrape of a heavy piece of furniture—stopped the biker, who straightened, his eyes leaving me and staring straight ahead, wider than a hillbilly in a boat in a swamp spotting a UFO. His gun was aimed upward, too, maybe at an alien. He stumbled forward and flopped onto Culver, who was outstretched on the bed post-bullet-in-the-head, the two men groin to groin, making an X, creating a new Kama Sutra position.

Framed in the doorway was Susan in her black puffy jacket, her eyes as wide as the dead biker's had been. She had her baby Glock in her feminine fist and a cute little curl of smoke was drifting from the barrel. I wondered if she had been smart enough to think it through: that holding that barrel flush to the biker's back would muffle the gunshot.

Or maybe it was just a happy accident.

I went over to her, guiding her inside, then peeking outside to see if any attention had been attracted. But the only other guests were down at the other end of the motel, in their rooms fucking or toking or watching the Gameshow Network, and that check-in shack wasn't looking any livelier than before, which is to say not lively at all.

That took a second, and then I shut all four of us in our snug little motel room.

"I…I got over here," Susan said, "as quick as I could. You didn't kill…?"

"No, that's our biker buddy's work, where Culver's concerned. You okay?"

"No," she said, and she was trembling. Shock can hit you even when no injury is involved. Of course, several injuries were involved here, just not to either one of us.

She managed to ask, "What did you find out?"

I had a hand on her shoulder. "That can wait. We need to get organized and quick." I took the gun from her. "Is this licensed?"

She shook her head. "No."

"Good girl," I said. "We need to leave it. I'll buy you a new one."

"I don't want one," she said numbly.

"Not right now. But you will."

She had gloves on, because of the cold, which was a lucky break. I put the Baby Glock in Culver's right hand, pressing it to make some fingerprints. The biker still had his Luger in hand, but I carefully removed the silencer and dropped it in a pocket of my jacket. I put the weapon back in the biker's hand.

"What are you doing?" she asked. She was weaving, drunk with disaster.

"I don't want this to look like a contract kill," I said. "It needs to read as some kind of half-assed lover's quarrel."

I wasn't wearing gloves, but except for the gun, which I'd wiped before replacing it in the biker's hand, I hadn't touched anything, not even the doorknob. So I was good.

"I think," she said, "I'm going to throw up."

"Don't. This room doesn't need any more DNA, particularly not yours." I put my arm around her shoulders and guided her toward the door. Again, I paused to peek outside and see if anybody was coming.

No.

As the cold hit us, the nine mil back in a jacket pocket, I said to her, "*That*'s tragedy."

We walked across to the Cadillac, my arm still around her, holding her tight, holding her close. I got her into the rider's seat and came around, got in, and started the vehicle.

We drove a while. I used the GPS to get us from Lyndale Avenue to I-35 West and headed south. I planned to find a truck stop after we were well out of Minneapolis where we could talk and clean up and regroup.

After a while, in the dashboard light, where she was sitting sideways in the seat, curled up like a fetus trying to get comfortable despite the seatbelt, she said, "Daddy?"

That startled me, her calling me that.

"I killed a man," she said.

"Honey," I told her, "I spilled more than that."

NINE

We'd been on the road less than forty-five minutes when I pulled off at the Clear Lake exit on I-35 and got fuel at Casey's. As I pumped gas, Susan sat up in the passenger seat and came awake in slow motion. The cold felt rather good to me, and the absence of falling snow was a plus for the drive ahead.

When I got behind the wheel, still in my jacket, I said, "We should stop for something to eat."

She looked at me like I suggested we should pitch a tent and build a campfire. "Are you kidding?"

"No. I'm hungry and we can both use a restroom break. There's a Perkins over there."

I drove over and parked in the mostly empty lot of the familiar green-roofed structure and she reluctantly went in with me, not bothering to zip up her jacket. The green and orange interior was no brighter than a doctor sticking his little flashlight in your eyes; nobody was here who wasn't staff except some truckers and a few old people, who either shouldn't have been up so late or were maybe just here early, beating the crowd.

We asked for a booth in back and got one. A pretty waitress in her early twenties who wasn't happy with the way her life was working out sullenly took our order. I got the 55-Plus Country Fried Steak with a Diet Coke and my shell-shocked daughter settled for coffee when I made her order *something*.

Our booth was isolated enough for our conversation not to raise eyebrows.

Her voice was uninflected and her expression blank but for sleepy eyes. "How many people *have* you killed?"

"No idea."

"Ballpark."

My Diet Coke came and her coffee, too. I sipped mine. She ignored hers.

I said, "Well, I had thirty-two confirmed kills in country."

"In what country?"

"Vietnam. That's how we referred to it. 'In country.' But there were plenty more unconfirmed."

"What about the five years of taking on contracts?"

I shrugged. "Figure thirteen."

She remained deadpan. "And the 'list' years?"

"Oh, I don't know. Twenty?"

"…How do you sleep?"

"Depends on if I've eaten pepperoni pizza. That can make for a rough night."

"You can joke about it."

"You think beating myself up would be better? You need to let it go, kid. That was self-defense back there."

Susan leaned forward, whispered, though nobody was close—there was hardly anybody here to *be* close.

She said, "I shot that man in the back."

"He was about to shoot me. Thank you, by the way. And he'd just killed your favorite interview subject."

She had a sip of coffee. Didn't look at me. "I don't know how you can be so casual about it."

"Really? After researching me for a hundred years?"

Now she looked at me. "I researched you, yes, but…it never seemed quite real to me. I was removed from it. It was a story."

"It wasn't a story where I was sitting."

"Journalism is what I mean." She slid out of the booth. "Excuse me."

She headed for the restrooms up front, past the glassed-in pies.

My food came and I was finished by the time she returned. Her eyes were as red as Culver's had been.

"Did you throw up?" I asked.

"No."

"Just sat there and cried."

"Yes."

I flipped a hand magnanimously. "Nothing wrong with getting it out of your system. As far as throwing up, if that doesn't happen right away, it probably won't."

"You speak from experience."

"In a firefight, there's no time to puke, and later you're on to the next thing. When you're a sniper up a tree? Throwing up would give your position away."

She closed her eyes. Opened them. Then: "How about your first contract? That make you sick to your stomach, at least?"

I shook my head. "Nope."

"Why not? Don't you feel *anything*?"

"About the other side in a shooting war? No. About people who got themselves in so much trouble somebody paid for them to be dead? No. About *anyone* I shoot in self-defense? Hell no."

She shifted in the seat. Sighed. "Who…who did I shoot, anyway?"

"I didn't get his name."

"No, I mean…what was that about? A jealous lover thing?"

"Really? You're one of America's top true-crime writers and that's what you came away with? You think that was just some random biker Culver met in a leather bar? That, my dear, was a honey trap till Culver's hubby wandered in and threw a wrench in the works."

Her eyes were tight. "He was a hired killer, the biker."

"Yes. You killed some lowlife who killed people for money. Does that make you feel better?"

"…You don't have to be an asshole."

"I try not to be, but it can be an effort. We're lucky Rough Trade didn't have a backup man watching. We could have got caught in some kind of crossfire."

She frowned, taking that in, the true-crime writer part of her kicking back in. "There's always two? Always a 'passive and an active'?"

"No. That's just how these brokers have traditionally done it. But you can hire a guy in a bar for a job if the money's right. And that can start at around fifty bucks."

She stared into her coffee. By the time I'd finished my meal, she'd drunk half of the cup.

The check came and I got out of the booth. "I'm going to pay for this."

"You think you *ever* will?"

What did she mean by that?

I left five bucks to encourage the waitress to go back and finish college, and headed for the register. Then I used the Men's while Susan milled in the entry area, staring into the night. I pushed open the door for her and she went out, and maybe her attitude was a little better. She zipped up the puffy black jacket, anyway. Our breaths plumed.

I opened the rear door and she looked at me funny.

"Stretch out and sleep," I said.

She nodded and climbed in. Stretched out on her side, facing away.

Whenever I'd check the rear-view mirror, or turn to peek, she'd be breathing heavy; when she rolled over to change sides, her eyes were closed and stayed that way. I left Sirius tuned to that easy-listening station, but kept the volume low and in front. The nearly four hours of driving that followed didn't bother me. I'd had enough Diet Coke for the caffeine to do the driving, and anyway I'm always a little stoked after surviving a shootout, even a minor one like that.

It wasn't four A.M. yet when we got back. I roused her and she sat up slowly, drugged from the depth of her own exhaustion. I helped her out and walked her to the front door, where she used her key and we went in and disappeared down the narrow hall to our respective bedrooms.

Neither of us said good night.

I woke at eleven-thirty or so and got myself showered, shaved and dressed. Sunlight was filtering its way through the many tall windows, patches of frost on the glass making odd abstractions out of shadows. They went well with the ersatz Wright house.

That big living room was designed to be lived in and included, near the kitchen, a dining room table, small and square and suitable for four, cherry wood with barrel chairs with vertical slatted backs. Susan was seated on one side with her laptop in front of her. Piles of files and papers were by the computer at left with a yellow legal pad and red pen at right.

This was not the shell-shocked girl of last night, rather the professional young woman who'd come calling on me three days ago…or was it a hundred years? Her blonde mane, carefully arranged in its casualness, was brushing the shoulders of a pale yellow silk blouse, and she was in loose black slacks. Her makeup was muted, typical for her, but that blood-red slash of lipstick was back, as were the spiky eyelashes.

She was typing something in as she said, "So you're not dead."

"Not that you'd notice."

"I thought you older men rose at the crack of dawn."

"Only when Dawn is a stewardess."

She glanced at me as I sat to her left. "Lame," she said. "And how old do you have to be to use 'stewardess,' anyway?"

"I don't know." I smiled at her. "Coffee, tea or Alzheimer's?"

That at least made her smile. "I already have coffee. Get yourself a Coke Zero and come back."

I did.

"You," I said, "look like you've been up a while."

"I slept in the car, remember, all the way home. I've been up most of the night."

"Well, you look fresh as a daisy anyway."

She grunted. "Christ, even your cliches are older than dirt."

I sipped Coke Zero. " 'Older than dirt' is a cliche unworthy of a writer of your stature. Is there breakfast or lunch or anything?"

"I thought you'd take me out for lunch, after I share what I've come up with. But you'll have to do better than Perkins."

"Denny's?"

A single laugh. "Okay, I've got folders on three possibilities for who might want you to be their valentine."

"In the St. Valentine's Day Massacre sense," I said, accepting the folders she held out to me. That may have been a 1929 reference, but it never got old.

She turned to me quite serious now. "Jack...Quarry...Dad?"

"Yes?"

The earnestness of her expression touched me somehow.

She said, "I can't guarantee I've zeroed in on whoever sent those two assassins to Sylvan Lake. You came up with thirty-three possibilities yourself last night."

"I did?"

She nodded. "The jobs you did for your Broker you put at thirteen. But also twenty potential victims of assassination who you helped by 'removing' those sent after them, then often getting rid of whoever had hired the job. So when I say thirty-three 'possibilities,' I mean sources of where the threat could come from. The actual number would be, well…staggering."

My turn to nod, as I sat there considering just how fucked I was.

"With a name from the Broker's list," I said, "on any given job, it could be a client who considers me a skeleton in the closet worth getting rid of…*or* it could be someone connected to a hit team I deactivated."

"I'll have to remember that one for the sequel," she said, with a sideways smile, " 'deactivation.' It makes 'liquidation' sound positively benign."

"Well, 'killed their asses' is so crude."

She outright laughed at that.

"Anyway," she said, "*you* lived this remarkable and, if I might be so bold, despicable life, not *me*. All I did was research it. But I have come up with three strong possibilities."

She outlined them for me. I will share them with you, reverting to the fictionalized names used previously.

"You never met him, to my knowledge," Susan said, reaching over and flipping open the first folder, "but I assume you're familiar with Montgomery Climer of Memphis, Tennessee."

"I am, and you're right," I said, looking at a picture of a tanned, greasy-haired, nastier version of Billy Bob Thornton, "I never met the man."

But I knew who Montgomery Climer was, all right—the impresario who'd revitalized the notorious *Climax* magazine, giving it a right-wing, blue-collar slant while beginning a successful national chain of Climax Lounges, merging gentlemen's clubs with adult shops peddling sex toys and lingerie.

She went on: "Montgomery's the brother of the late Vernon Climer, who was their cousin Max Climer's partner in creating

Climax magazine—an empire built out of a flier for their local strip clubs in the '70s."

"I'd argue," I said, "that it was an empire built on the American male's childish fascination with gynecological photography. But what do I know?"

She smirked at that. "Would it surprise you to learn there are those who consider you almost certainly responsible for the death of Montgomery Climer's brother Vernon? You took credit for it in one of your 'novels,' after all."

"It becomes increasingly obvious," I said, "that I've been indiscreet. But in my defense, I was pretty well off the grid at the time."

"Not enough so that a skilled true-crime writer," she reminded me, "couldn't track you down."

"Ouch," I said.

Her eyebrows rose. "Shall we move on?"

"Why not."

She flipped open the next folder and directed me to an unpleasant photograph of an old boy with more wrinkles than a Shar Pei and the flat head, big eyes, and wide thin mouth of a lizard.

"In Biloxi, Mississippi," she said, "there's a rather elderly gentleman named Theodore Brunner—known as 'Terrible Theo' in his less geriatric days. His brother was one Alex Brunner, a nasty piece of work by all accounts, who was shot in his office by, presumably, gangland rivals. A minor massacre, actually."

"Three isn't a massacre. Three is hardly trying."

"Perhaps. But Theo owns one of Biloxi's few surviving strip clubs from the '70s era, sporting the classy name 'Bottoms Up.' Actually, it's likely to close for good at the end of the summer season. They took a beating during the pandemic."

I shrugged. "I never met Theo Brunner, but I'm confident he's terrible. What does it have to do with me?"

But of course I sort of already knew.

She said, "There's a general belief in the world of the Dixie Mafia—it turned up in half a dozen interviews I conducted with mob figures from that era—that you were responsible for that tiny little massacre that included Alex Brunner back in the '80s. You'll note that we have a recurring theme."

"Strip clubs?"

"Revenge. Terrible Theo might well want you dead, if he buys the rumors. It's just an assumption on my part, I grant you. Mr. Brunner has never agreed to an interview. But word among his cronies is, once 'Bottoms Up' bottoms out, he will retire to Florida. So he may want to tidy the books up before he closes up shop. Settle a score or two."

"Revenge is one recurring theme," I said. "Pissed-off family members is another."

"Well, you know what they say."

"What's that?"

"You can't choose your relatives."

Score one for the ungrateful child.

"But," she said, "our final candidate in the who-wants-to-treat-you-to-the-dish-best-served cold, Quarry, is someone you probably haven't heard a whisper about. And this one is right here in the Quad Cities."

Where was a drumroll when you needed one?

She flipped the last folder to an African American in a sharp business suit—Armani?—handsome in a Sam Cooke kind of way, if Sam had made it to his forties.

"Jeffrey Kinman," she said. "Mean anything?"

"No idea who this is."

She flipped another photo, this time to an African-American

woman in her fifties, beautifully dressed, somberly smiling, rather lovely.

"How about *Donna* Kinman?" Susan asked. "Ring a distant bell maybe?"

"No. Not the faintest ding."

"What if I said her late husband was *Arnold* Kinman?"

I frowned, memories stirring. "He was the manager at the Concort Inn, way back when—a partner in the place. The Concort was mostly the Broker's, though, as far as I ever knew. And it's still around—we drove right past it getting here."

She was nodding. "Even now, the Concort is one of the most successful hotels in the area—across from, and affiliated with, the Mississippi Queen Casino."

This wasn't anything I'd kept close tabs on, but *that* bell was finally dinging. "Didn't Arnold Kinman wind up *owning* the Concort?"

She gave me one last, decisive nod. "Your 'Broker' owned fifty-one percent of the hotel, and Kinman forty-nine. Arnold inherited two percent of the Broker's share, giving him control. Why this generosity on the partner's part, I haven't been able to determine. Local talk is they were just great friends."

That sounded wrong. "Kinman died, didn't he, quite a while ago?"

"Yes," she said, "in the early '90s, and his wife Donna took over. That caused some ripples locally, back then."

"Why?"

"She was an African American who'd been employed in housekeeping in the hotel before she and Arnold married. But she went on to take Business Administration at Augustana College. When she died a few years ago, their son Jeffrey, who'd been working with her for years, took over all their business interests. He's about my age, maybe a little older.

Mississippi Queen, Inc. is a publicly traded company now, with eight casinos in multiple states."

I was shaking my head. "What makes Jeffrey Kinman somebody who'd want *me* dead?"

"I admit I can't make much of a case for it. Still, it wouldn't be hard for anybody in the Quad Cities to think 'Quarry' was responsible for the death of the respected hotelier you call the Broker. And where would the Kinmans have been without him?"

I huffed a laugh. "Where would they be without me? I got them that hotel."

She sat back. "So where do we go from here?"

I already knew. "I'm going to follow the Memphis and Biloxi leads myself."

"If I were *with* you," she said, gesturing with an open hand, "I could play the true-crime writer role and—"

"You need to do that right here in the Cities. Have you ever had contact with Jeffrey Kinman about your *Sniper* sequel?"

She shook her head. "A few preliminary phone calls. He seems willing to talk, but we haven't worked out a time."

"Do so. Dog his heels if you have to. Do whatever research you can do on him locally, really hit up your QC media sources, and we'll compare notes when I get back."

She was frowning. "What if these all turn out to be dead ends?"

"We keep trying, till *I'm* dead…which would be the end. More coffee?"

TEN

I had those several fake IDs with me but no credit cards to back them up, while my Sylvan Lake identity had both. Nothing had made it to the national press about the killings up north, and why would it? And if on the very long shot that somebody in that neck of the literal woods decided I was a person of interest or even a suspect, why would that extend beyond Minnesota state lines? I'd been in Minnesota yesterday and nothing about any of it was in the media there.

This made me comfortable, or anyway comfortable enough, to avoid a twelve-hour car ride from Davenport to Biloxi by buying an airline ticket in my regular identity. A nonstop flight at 2:45 that afternoon would get me there by quarter after five.

This allowed time for a father-and-daughter lunch at Miss Mamie's, a Cajun-style place near the airport. Susan brought her laptop along and I had her search some names. One was Luann Lloyd. That took a while because Lloyd was her maiden name and she was Luann Crawford now—seemed she was the owner and manager of the Fantasy Sweets, a honeymoon and trysting destination that had been on the Biloxi strip half a lifetime ago. The pictures on Yelp looked much the same and the reviews called the place a hoot. Good for her.

The Bottoms Up, the Net told me, had been in the same location since it opened in 1968. Very little turned up about its owner, Theodore Brunner, except the club itself, those few mentions representing probably half-hearted occasional efforts at raids by paid-off cops.

Susan dropped me off at the Moline airport at a quarter till two. She didn't come in to see me off, avoiding an awkward moment. Hug? Kiss on the cheek? Handshake? Simple wave? Just turn and go?

Neither of us needed that kind of fucking pressure. So we settled for her giving me the show biz wish: "Break a leg." And me saying, "I'll try to make it somebody else's."

When I stepped outside the Gulfport–Biloxi International Airport, suitcase in hand, military jacket over an arm, the area's inevitable muggy weather was waiting. It was in the fifties and should have felt cool, but it didn't.

I caught a cab, making sure I got an older guy. He was black and grizzled and friendly, but didn't ask any questions about why I wanted to be taken to the nearest used car dealer who might sell me an acceptable vehicle for under two grand.

It did make him laugh, though. "Didn't think my damn drivin' sucked *that* bad."

"There's a twenty buck tip in it," I said, "if you don't show me too much scenery."

But scenery kicked in right away, with trees in and around various businesses, winter-skeletal but for the firs. We passed a Salvation Army thrift shop and a liquor store, then pulled in at a low-slung metal building on Tennessee Avenue that didn't even bother to say what it was. Beater used cars with prices on the inside of windshields in soap—a little-seen technique these days—were lined up outside along the unmarked building.

"Try an' find yourself one," the cabbie said, "that'll make it out of the lot."

I handed him thirty bucks, covering the seven-minute ride and the tip, and he was gone in a cloud of gravel dust.

A black guy of maybe sixty in coveralls and short white hair and a short white beard approached. "Fix you up with a sweet ride," he said with a pickpocket's grin.

"My grandson's in high school," I said. "I want something, anything that will get him around. But if it breaks down on him out of the gate, I'll come around and burn this place down."

I was grinning as I said that, and he chuckled at my joke, suspecting it might not be one.

"Well," he drawled, "it's a metal buildin', so good luck. What you got to spend?"

"A grand."

He suggested a beige 1990 Oldsmobile Eighty-Eight Royale with "less miles per year than most." That turned out to be just over 200,000. But the engine sounded fine, and the guy in coveralls said he'd been a mechanic for thirty-seven years and serviced this puppy himself.

We breezed through the Bill of Sale with me using one of my fake IDs and then he got his grand and I got my sweet ride. I say that with tongue in cheek, but it really was a lot of car for the money. I'm sure my grandson will love it.

The jaunt from the airport into Biloxi held few familiar landmarks after so much time. On Hewes Avenue it was wintry trees and commercial here and residential there, and then on East Beach Blvd came more trees and condos and now and then a patch of the residue of the old strip, a Waffle House, a Quality Inn, a souvenir shop, another Waffle house, a casino hotel, a seafood joint, a Waffle House....

The Fantasy Sweets ("Your Wish is Our Command!") hadn't changed much at all, which must have required considerable upkeep effort. The brown-trimmed white stucco structure, vaguely Tudor if less so than the late Wesley Culver's Minneapolis digs, had added a carport, but that was about it.

I left my new 1990 car in the front lot and entered the small lobby with its homey gas fireplace. Where a wall of *Reader's Digest* condensed books had been now resided a small table with coffee and condiments over which photos of the various fantasy suites loomed—castle, bridal, Roman, space capsule, igloo, jungle, same as decades before, but several new ones, circus, cowboy, hippie.

The bulk of the hotel in the '70s, when I last set foot in this place, was standard rooms. I lugged in my small suitcase and figured this time of year I'd have no trouble getting a room— the lack of vehicles in the parking lot indicated as much and the woman at the modest check-in desk confirmed it.

In her fifties, Marla (as her gold metal name tag identified her) was a little heavy but very pretty, her hair an artificial but not unbecoming red. She first ascertained I was not in the market for one of the fantasy "sweets" and accommodated my request for a room off the pool. I used my Sylvan ID and Visa card, checking in.

In the little office behind her, another woman was at a computer. She was a brunette, attractively middle-aged, nicely coiffed and with makeup that knew when to quit.

At my age, well-preserved women at their age were a constant fantasy.

"Do you need help with your bags?" Marla asked.

I had the feeling that, in the off-season anyway, she'd probably be the one doing that, with the gal in the little office coming up to fill in at the front desk.

"No," I said, hefting the small suitcase, "this is all I have with me. I understand Mrs. Crawford is still the manager here."

The redhead nodded. She had green eyes. She looked like the fourth-grade teacher boys loved but didn't know why. "Yes, she is." Her head bobbed behind her. "But this is not her office."

That seemed calculated to give and withhold information at the same time.

I said, "Luann and I are old friends. I'd really like to say hello. Could I leave her a note...?"

She was sizing me up. "You can. But I could give her a call and let her know you're staying with us."

"Would you? I'll be in my room for an hour, at least, before going out to get something to eat. Tell her that her old friend Johnny is here. Say Johnny from the Tropical."

Since I'd checked in with the Sylvan Lake identity, that first name was consistent.

"I'll do that, Mr. Keller," Marla said. "Would you like a map of the facility? And we do give tours of the 'Sweets' on request, those that aren't occupied...and many aren't this time of year."

"No, I can follow the signs," I said, and I also remembered my way around, at least well enough.

My non-"Sweet" room was fine, something out of a Comfort Inn or Courtyard Marriott, its most appealing feature the sliding door onto the swimming pool area. I got into my trunks and reflected on whether I needed to wrap my nine mil in my towel, then decided against it. No one knew I was here except Marla.

Actually, somebody else did.

I'd barely swum a lap in the warm pool when the click of high heels in the high-chambered echoey space announced a female caller. I swam over to the side and, I admit it, my mouth dropped open.

Luann Crawford, as she was now known, was walking over to me in the slightly foggy air of a pool room kept too warm, looking utterly the same and wholly different.

By which I mean, she was still a slenderly shapely woman, though now in her early sixties, her hair a startling white now, and her features still baby-doll pretty dominated by big blue eyes. But her apparel told me I was looking at a professional woman, and certainly not the profession she was in when I first met her—she wore a beautifully tailored gray pantsuit and a white silk blouse with a bow at the neck.

I pulled myself out of the pool and sat there dripping, an agape ape. "You got here fast."

She was looming over me like a mirage manufactured from my memories. "My office is on site, in back. You got kind of old, but I've seen worse."

"Thank you?"

She bent at the knees and her smile was barely discernible. I could see years on her face now, but they hadn't done any harm. "Dry off and get dressed. I'll take you out to dinner."

Mary Mahoney's—still in the Old French House, a white-clapboard New Orleans-style mansion on Rue Magnolia—had changed even less than Luann. We sat at a white-linen-covered table on white chairs; the walls were pale yellow and framed pictures of pelicans rode the walls.

We ordered—Veal Antonio for me, Sisters of the Sea Au Gratin for her—then shared an order of fried green tomatoes with crabmeat and crawfish.

"Back to blonde, I see," I said.

She delicately forked some tomato. "Brunette didn't last long. But this isn't blonde."

"No?"

"It's white. And well-earned."

"If you've had work done, I hope you tipped the doctor. You look fuckin' great."

"You always had a classy way with words, Johnny."

I grinned. "My God, a sense of humor. They didn't teach you that in night school."

She smiled. "You gave me my first lessons. So what brings

you here? It's only been forty years since you last stopped by."

"Don't exaggerate. Barely thirty-eight."

Our food arrived.

I said, "Let's just enjoy each other's company. Small talk first. We can go big later."

She nodded and we dined like civilized people. She had been married three times, and the first two hadn't worked. They both, she said, married her for her money.

"How much money do you have, anyway?"

"Enough to pay for this meal," she said teasingly, "if you're worrying I'll stick you with it."

I chuckled, had a bite of veal. "I think maybe I liked you better *without* a sense of humor."

She laughed a little. "That was what was wrong with my second husband—he didn't have one. The first was mobbed up. I didn't divorce him, somebody shot him."

"Not me! I have an alibi…or I'll work one up."

Another small laugh, then a shake of the head. "My second husband owned an insurance agency and I thought he was well-off, but he was stealing from his clients and I was his biggest mark, his way of buying himself out of a hole. But at least I got a kid out of it. A good one."

"Yeah?"

"A boy. A son. Grown man, now. A lawyer in Atlanta."

I had another bite. Just as good as I remembered it. "What about *Mister* Crawford?"

"Husband number three? He was ten years older than me, a widower I met. We had some nice years. He dropped dead just over there."

She pointed to a table across the room.

"Sorry," I said.

"Yeah. Thanks."

"I hope he wasn't having the Veal Antonio."

She started laughing and about choked on her bite of shrimp and crabmeat.

"I take it back," I said. "I like you even *better* with a sense of humor."

We shared a piece of key lime pie, coffee with hers, iced tea for me.

I asked, "Whatever happened to those floppy disks from Alex Brunner's safe?"

"One went to a top politician, the other to a Dixie Mafia biggie. I told them both I didn't keep copies."

"Which meant you might have."

She nodded. "But I didn't ask for money or favors. And doors opened up. Like magic."

"Abracadabra."

Her head tilted. "So what's this about, Johnny?"

I told her, briefly, quietly, as there was no need to scare our few fellow diners. I explained that I was in the position she'd been in the last time I was in Biloxi. Somebody wanted me dead and a hit team had been sent.

She frowned in concern. "And you think Theo Brunner hired it?"

"He may have. I could be grasping at straws."

She sipped her coffee. "He's a good candidate. He might be in a mood to settle scores. The fact is, I'm not surprised by any of what you've said."

"No?"

She nodded. "I may have gone higher brow since you saw me, but I'm still tuned in to the lowlifes."

"I notice you're giving some of your ex-strippers a second career working at the 'Sweets.'"

She nodded, the white hair bouncing. "I am. I hired a bunch

of them to work at all our locations—we have three more, you know. Illinois, Arkansas, Florida. Anyway, word's gotten around that I hired Alex Brunner's killing, and that the same mysterious man suspected of several other 'mob-related' murders in Biloxi ten years before that, had been an associate of mine."

"We associated, all right."

The big blue eyes trained themselves on me. "Frankly, my first thought when I got your message? That you were here to tell me I've been marked for murder myself. Again."

"Once every forty years. Only we switch places this time. But I have to admit—I haven't figured out how to confront this old buzzard. If I stick a gun in his yap, he might just croak on me."

"You do need refining, Johnny. You just haven't grown. Tell me—do you think you could pass for an attorney?"

"Not in this," I said, gesturing to my long-sleeve t-shirt and jeans.

"We'll do something about that," she said, "on our way to Bottoms Up."

Unlike Luann, and Fantasy Sweets, Bottoms Up *had* changed, and not for the better. The one-and-a-half-story brown-brick building, squatting in a graveled parking lot, shedding dark roof tiles, had an unstable look, like it had been lifted by a tornado and dropped there. The lot had half a dozen cars out front and half a dozen more out back, probably employee ones.

Luann pulled in her money-green Lexus, a redundant statement if ever there was one. Of course I looked like money, too, in the Ralph Lauren off-the-rack suit she'd bought me at the Edgewater Mall Men's Wearhouse.

Just as hers was the only Lexus in the parking lot, mine was the only suit in Bottoms Up, where a handful of airmen and college boys and blue-collar guys sat along the edges of a stage where two lackluster strippers, both white, one blonde, one brunette, down to their g-strings, competed to see who had better tattoos and less cellulite. Hip hop was booming. Don't ask me what.

A bouncer, a big black guy in red sweats that stood out in the near dark—blue lighting from the overhead stage spots provided the only illumination—slouched against a wall.

All this was going on centrally while a few lap dances along the walls at tables were underway and a bartender who seemed qualified to back up that lone bouncer was pouring himself a drink. He was wearing a white tuxedo shirt, unbuttoned half-way down to an undershirt, and he either needed a shave or his face could use scrubbing.

Stale beer and fresh puke mingled in their unique yet familiar bouquet. That I'd been in too many places like this was not a good reflection on my time on the planet.

The bartender noticed Luann and her presence visibly startled him—this might have been one of those rare unscheduled police raids.

We went over to him. He had the look of a man realizing he was about to be served a summons. That was a beard, by the way, not that his face couldn't have used scrubbing. His eyes were tiny and his jowls weren't.

"Yeah?" he asked us accusatively.

"I'm Luann Crawford."

"I know."

"I assume your boss is here. He always is. Theo Brunner?"

"I know his name. He's in."

"I want to see him."

"I'm *workin'*, lady!"

I leaned in and said, "Well, take a breather. We'll hold down the fort."

He gave me a careful look. I might have been an old guy in a new suit, but he saw something there.

Like a girl at a dance rebuffed on a ladies' choice, he huffed off. We held down the fort. No Indians turned up. The bartender returned.

"Mr. Brunner," the bartender said. "Theo Brunner?"

"I know his name," Luann said dryly.

I felt so proud of her.

"He'll see you," the bartender said, and gestured vaguely toward the Sitters and Setters, as if one of those doors would be Brunner's office. We went in that direction and discovered a hall past the restrooms leading to a door that said NO ENTRY. This took us by a door from which another pair of tired strippers, wearing bikinis that would soon be gone, trudged wearily out. One had needle marks and bruises, the other just bruises.

We approached NO ENTRY. Luann looked at me and I looked at her.

"Nothing ventured," I said.

She knocked.

"*Yeah!*"

The voice came thick, like somebody's tongue was swollen.

I opened the door for her and followed her in. The office was bigger than a closet, which is about all I can say about or for it. Behind a desk was a flabbily obese man in a brown suit—there were two of us in off-the-rack jobs now, his threads enough to make me wonder if Robert Hall was still in business. His features had to work to be seen in a stack of wrinkles, a squeeze box un-squeezed. His head was a kind of upside-down cone with wisps of hair on top, like a witch's mole. His eyes were light blue and might have been pretty on a young woman, minus the rheumy matter, and his chin jutted like it was trying to escape.

Let me point out that he did not wear a tie, making me the

more dapper of the men here. A couple of folding chairs were just waiting to be pulled in front of the old desk, one foot of which was broken off, with its remains resting on some stacked phone books from before land-lines got unpopular.

Theodore Brunner was smoking a cigar and drinking beer from a pilsner, a glass pitcher with about another glass worth in it resting on a desk cluttered with papers and photos with stripper applications. A lumpy couch along a wall summoned unpleasant images.

"To what do I owe this honor?" he asked Luann, as she sat. His teeth were dark yellow in the aperture under his tumor of a nose.

We sat.

He sneered at me. "And who is this asshole?"

"My attorney," she said, not putting a name to it. "He came up from Florida."

He swatted the air in my direction. "Yeah, yeah, right, you got one of those Fantasy Soots down there too, don't you. Maybe I'll drop by when I retire, if the wife puts up with it."

He had a wife. Oh my fucking God.

"I want to make you an offer, Mr. Brunner."

"Come on, Luann. We go back. Way back. You was in the stripper trade before I was. You look like you could still get a guy hot enough to stick a dollar in your skivvies. Call me Theo."

"Thank you for the compliment, Theo."

"My pleasure. What can I do you for?"

She shrugged. "Business has been off. Covid hit all of us hard. Rumor has it you really *are* thinking of a Florida move."

Coyly he said, "And if I am?"

"You'll need to be selling this property. Meaning no offense, it's clear your heart isn't in the game anymore. The place is awfully rundown. Again, no offense."

"None the fuck taken. What's your point?"

"I'd like to buy you out."

He grunted a laugh. "What, and remodel?"

She shook her head, smiled a little. "No, tear it down. Come on, Theo. You know this lot is worth much more with your business not on it. I'm prepared to make a generous offer."

He flicked cigar ash on the floor. "You're too late, honey. I got three prime bids I'm considering."

She looked at him unblinkingly. "How much is the best one?"

A tiny yellow grin. "That would not be kosher, business-wise. Ethics and such like."

She sat forward. "How much, Theo, is the top offer? I can ask around and find out easy enough."

He sat back. "There's half a mil on the table, sweet cheeks."

She glanced at me. I shrugged.

Then she said, "I'll go three quarters of a mil. That's seven hundred and fifty thousand dollars, Theo."

His eyes got so wide they almost popped out of the wrinkles. "That's a legit offer?"

"It's a legit offer. My lawyer here will draw up the papers and get them back to you tomorrow. But I want to move fast."

He fidgeted in his chair. "Okay. Okay! Sure. We go way back, like I said. I won't even fuckin' haggle! You have bought yourself a goddamn strip club, cutie."

She lifted a forefinger. "One thing."

He frowned. "What thing?"

Luann opened a hand like a flower blossoming. "There are rumors about me...pertaining to you, or anyway your late brother. He and I had some difficulties, trying to work out a similar deal, a long time ago."

"I remember that," he admitted, gazing suspiciously at her.

"And I heard a disturbing rumor recently," she said, leaning forward, the white arcs of her hair swinging like twin scythes, "that you hold me responsible for his death, years ago. For his…killing."

"No! Of course not—where did you hear such a thing?"

"I still have my sources, Theo. The story is that a young man who worked for Jack Killian…who once owned this very club, back in its '70s heyday…was a lover of mine. And that he made that raid on your brother's penthouse."

"I don't think that! Not in the least! That's crazy. Everybody knows it was Dixie Mafia wiseguys. Them greedy bastards tryin' to take over."

Her head tilted to one side, the arcs swinging again. "Well, it did happen when Alex, rest his soul, was making offers to buy me out. Back when I still had Lolita's?"

He held fat palms up as if giving himself up. "That's a dumb fuckin' rumor, it's people talkin' outa their ass."

She stood. "So we're cool? We have a deal?"

He somehow got himself upright and stuck out a pudgy hand. "We have a deal. We're cool."

She shook it, nodded, gathered her purse.

I nodded to him, saying, "You'll hear from me, Mr. Brunner," and we went out.

The strippers we'd passed in the hall were buck naked on stage now. Another Hip Hop "song" was booming.

In the Lexus, in the parking lot, she used a handiwipe on her hands, looked over at me from behind the wheel, and asked, "So? What do you think?"

"I think his pointy head is swimming with your seven-hundred-and-fifty grand. What do you think?"

"I agree."

I squinted at her. "You really going to buy that property? I mean…*could* you?"

"I could. But half a mil is all it's worth. He didn't seem to recognize you, and if he organized a hit with you as the target, you'd think he would."

"Thanks for this, Luann."

"Don't mention it. Come on back to the hotel. I'm going to upgrade your room...."

ELEVEN

The ceiling was plastered with black-light posters—Jimi Hendrix haloed in fiery yellow/green against a sea of purple, an orange John Lennon face in granny glasses emerging from an ebony void, a purple-and-green Cheshire Cat encouraging us to smile, Mr. Natural in red with green boots, keepin' on truckin' across a blue globe.…

One deep purple wall bore a giant green-graduated-to-purple peace symbol, another a rainbow mushroom saying EAT ME, while opposite an array of framed LP covers stared back—*Sgt. Pepper, Pet Sounds, Surrealistic Pillow, Blonde on Blonde, Electric Ladyland, Their Satanic Majesties*. The windows wore tie-dye blackout curtains and any space left on the purple walls had a black-and-white poster of a rock legend—Blind Faith, Janis Joplin, Vanilla Fudge, Led Zeppelin. The periphery was lined with low-slung wall-hugging dark purple couches bearing multi-color, vari-designed pillows, while the floor was carpeted in wide shag stripes of orange, cream and yellow. On either side as you entered, Oriental carpets were hung, opposite a big low-riding waterbed, purple with magenta pillows and a black faux leather headboard, right smack in the middle of the Hippie Sweet, its literal centerpiece.

"Groovy," I said.

"I was never a hippie," Luann admitted. She was still in her gray pantsuit and I in my Ralph Lauren. We had just stepped into this world. "But it's fun, isn't it?"

I hadn't been a hippie, either, spending much of those years overseas. But the counterculture had been all around me. I'd been to the Whiskey A Go Go in L.A. and the drug scene in Vietnam rivaled anything stateside, though it had never been my thing.

I tossed my suitcase (which looked as out of place as we did) on the waterbed and it bobbed gently while the bed gently sloshed. Black nightstands bore lava lamps, neither turned on at the moment, though I imagined many guests to this "Sweet" had been. I checked out the bathroom and found it less aggressively decorated—just a Woodstock toilet seat and a framed TAKE A BATH YOU DIRTY HIPPIE poster hovering over a Jacuzzi.

"This isn't your only option, of course," Luann said. "Only two suites are occupied right now. You can go cowboy or spaceman or ringmaster."

"More choice these days."

She nodded. "I think we only had six 'Sweets' when you were here back…God, in the '70s."

"You were just an occasional employee at the time."

"That's a nice way to say I did a good share of my hooking out of here. Well, when I sold Lolita's, a hotel bought me out. Wasn't unlike what I was proposing to our friend Theo. But I had prime real estate, and with the proceeds was able to buy the Sweets."

"Trading up."

She nodded, arms folded, smiling a little. "It was a natural progression, moving from hooking and stripping to using the money you liberated for me. Enabled me to buy Lolita's. From there to here, it fell nicely into place, and of course I expanded to other cities."

I slipped an arm around her. "If it's not patronizing of me to say…I'm proud of you."

Her smile was modest—those pretty little white teeth remaining in hiding—but it was a lovely thing. So was she.

"I like hearing you say that, Johnny. So—shall we continue our magical mystery tour, or get off the magic bus right here?"

I said, "This room will do fine. It's a hoot."

"They're *all* hoots," she said, with a shrug, "but this one especially. I have an embarrassing admission to make."

"What's that?"

She gestured to the suite's low-slung centerpiece. "I've never had a chance to try out this waterbed."

"I've, uh, slept on a waterbed a few times. It's interesting."

She gave me a little sideways look. "Maybe you'd like some company tonight."

"Maybe I would. You have anybody in mind?"

"I do."

We'd been standing there taking it all in, but now she led me to one of those couches along the wall and sat me down. The lighting was subdued, but I don't think that had much if anything to do with the appraisal I made of her charms at this advanced age, which she shared with me by doing a striptease that in my opinion easily surpassed anything Lolita's much less Bottoms Up had to offer.

First, however, she slipped into the bathroom and sealed herself in for a few minutes. I thought she might emerge naked, but she was still fully clothed. She came over and switched on the lava lamp on her side of the waterbed, then strutted around and switched on mine. Then she killed the overhead lighting.

She went over to a mini-jukebox CD player on a little stand under the wall of LP covers and touched some keys and Steppenwolf's "Magic Carpet Ride" ignited with enough punch to make me suspect this was a soundproofed room. With the total lack of self-consciousness of a girl who'd become a stripper at thirteen, she began to do a little pony dance, the arcs of white hair swinging, lost in herself; she slipped off the pantsuit jacket, tossed it, then kicked away her low-riding heels and shimmied out of the pants, exposing sheer panties.

She resumed her little dance as she unbuttoned the silk blouse and eased it from her shoulders and flung it carelessly as well. She was more fully breasted at this age, though the rest of her figure was as slender as ever, if more muscular, probably due to working out being a part of how she maintained a beauty that struck me now as timeless.

"Afraid there's only so much I can do," she said, as she danced before me, slowing a bit, "without a pole."

"I can remedy that."

She laughed and stepped out of the sheer panties and used their elastic to snap them at me, slingshot style, and they bounced off my chest to join her scattered clothing on the shag carpet. Her brown bush wasn't trimmed back, appropriately enough for the hippie-era setting; it was a jungle tuft rejecting the pretense that bald is better.

"Magic Carpet Ride" was hitting its psychedelic stride, where that driving beat gave away to something faster, the song itself abandoned for improvisation and sheer hypnotic noise. She swayed over to the wall and hit another switch and overhead UV black light came on, and the posters on the ceiling came alive, as if the past were pushing through the present. Her dancing became more free-form, arms waving slowly, hips swinging and grinding, a reminder of how good she had once been on stage, and if I'd had a million dollars I'd have stuffed it in her g-string only she wasn't wearing one.

And then the beautiful naked woman stood motionless before me under the black light, her lips glowing red and her nipples the same, explaining her brief visit to the bathroom. A lipstick arrow on her tummy pointed to her bush. As if I needed help to know the way....

Then that red mouth floated over and invisible hands took off my suitcoat and pitched it, unbuttoned my shirt and pitched that, too. Then she unzipped my pants and then they and my shorts were at my ankles and she knelt before me, her head descending until it was this bobbing thing smearing my dick with lipstick, red under the black light, slow, slower, fast, faster. When she got me within moments of climax, she danced away giggling and hit another switch and a strobe light kicked in.

A hand was dragging me and then I was on my back on the waterbed and she was on top, my lips licking the red off her nipples, my hands guiding the firm round bottom, her move-ment fragmented by the strobe, the undulation of the water below merging with the rhythm and bounce of the beauty riding me, her red-tipped breasts swaying, and frankly it didn't take long.

She kissed me and bounced off the bed, moving toward the light switches, picking up clothing like flowers in May as she went. How firm and supple her body looked, in her sixties—and this was a sixties room, wasn't it?—simply amazing. She dialed the lighting down and ran off into the bathroom. The red of the lava lamps with their continuous, lugubrious motion of wax blobs rising within rocket-like aluminum-cased shafts, created lulling shadows.

I pulled on my boxers, got under the covers and fell asleep, lulled also by the waterbed's motion, but then she was suddenly back, crawling onto the bed, wearing a Fantasy Sweets-crested bathrobe.

"How about the floor next time?" I asked her.

"No." She got under the covers. "You don't ever want to make love on a hotel room floor. Trust me. Takes extra cleaning to get away with the black light. You can come home with me. We can do it now if you like."

"Where do you live?"

"Same place on Father Ryan. It's worth a fortune now. I only make good investments, you know, and it's close to work."

"Next visit."

"Don't wait forty years."

"Thirty-eight."

"That either."

The door came open with a splintering crack that took the night latch with it and the silhouette of a big man was poised against the hallway light. I pushed Luann off onto the floor on her side of the bed, and rolled back over onto mine as two silenced gunshots coughed and punctured the waterbed's covers and skin and immediately the world changed under me and I began to sink. The silhouette moved into the darkness and another, shorter, fatter silhouette followed and then the lights came on and it was the unshaven bartender in a BOTTOMS UP black sweatshirt and Theo Brunner in his baggy brown suit and baggy yellow skin and unending corpulence and I grabbed the lava lamp by the glass shaft, ignoring the heat, yanking it hard enough to pull its cord from the socket, and I hurled the thing, hard, at the bartender.

It hit him in the forehead, making a satisfying *klonk*, and his eyes opened very wide and he knelt, swayed, then fell.

"Freddy!" Theo yelled, hovering over the fallen bartender.

I was getting in my suitcase, which was at my bedside, leaning off the shifting waterbed to do so and clawing for the nine mil. Theo was lumbering over with an automatic almost as fat as he was. His obscenely wrinkled face managed an unmistakable expression of displeasure.

"I *recognized* you, you prick!" he said, baring those awful yellow teeth. "It was a long fuckin' time ago, but I *saw* you with Killian in '72! You killed my brother!"

"No!" Luann said from the floor. "*I* killed him!"

Theo's attention went to her, and she wasn't lying in the sense that she *had* bid the job done, but the misleading confession served its purpose because it gave me time to get the nine mil out and shoot that fat fuck.

Normally I would have gone for a head shot, but I had my reasons for plugging him in the belly, and not just that it was an easy target. He did an uncoordinated dance, and teetered, then fell hard on his back, shaking everything not nailed down. The splashing gore on the wall by a hanging Oriental carpet fit in fine with the psychedelic theme.

I got out of bed and went over there, taking a pillow with me. The bartender was unconscious or maybe dead. The other big slob on his back had his fingers on his belly trying to hold the blood in, but it was bubbling through and starting to soak his shirt and suitcoat.

"You're going to die," I said. "The question is whether you go gut-shot, which could take a while. I'll give you an early retirement if you level with me."

"Wh…wh…wha…."

"Did you hire it?"

"Hi…er…hi…er…wha…?"

"The hit on me."

His frown had more than abject pain in it—confusion colored it. He clearly did not know what the fuck I was talking about. That was good enough for me. I put the pillow over his face and buried the nine mil barrel in it and fired one into that pointy skull.

"Johnny!" Luann cried.

I turned and the bartender was awake and coming at me. He'd lost his gun when I clocked him with the lava lamp, and now, when he sacked me, mine went flying. That waterbed was close to the ground and his tackle took me onto it, on my back, and the thing was already leaking badly.

He was a big man, bigger than me, and younger than me, *way* the fuck younger than me, but when I grabbed his balls and squeezed, size and age were no longer factors. He yelled like the home team made a touchdown and I pushed him off me and held him down on top of that big oozing bag of a mattress and used his weight to make that water flow faster, a rip forming between bullet holes. He was gurgling but managing to spit and catch non-liquid breaths.

"Luann! Help!"

She climbed onto the bed and helped me hold him down. It took a while and he bucked and wriggled and splashed and flailed, but all of it slowed and finally he went limp and he wasn't faking: he had drowned, all right.

I was breathing hard and so was Luann. It was like we'd been fucking again. She climbed off her side of the dying waterbed and I climbed off mine and we looked across the dead floating man between us.

"That was a first for me," she said, wide-eyed.

"Not me," I said. "First time I needed a girl's help, though."

That made her laugh.

I liked her so much better with a sense of humor.

At the front desk, the woman who had checked me in, Marla, had been working alone. She'd been grabbed by the bartender and bound into a chair in the small office, and gagged, with duct tape. This was where Luann hiring ex-strippers came in handy—Marla understood that Luann and I would handle this. No police, and certainly no police report.

A bonus in Marla's paycheck was strongly implied.

On Theo's body I had found a key card that Luann identified

as a master. And that key card, which was updated daily, was missing at the front desk.

The hallway with the Hippie Sweet had no other guests, so that wasn't a problem. The empty room below the suite would have water damage from above, and likely bullet holes in the ceiling. Luann would get that discreetly taken care of. Ditto the Hippie Sweet itself. She still had, after all these years, connections.

But there were things we needed to deal with now. Right now. Tonight.

Back in our dry clothes, looking rumpled in our business attire, as if things had gotten out of hand at the Christmas party, we rounded up a laundry cart. Together we piled Theo and his bartender into the cart, covered them with dirty sheets and towels, which I told her would have to be burned later, and checked our guests out via the service elevator. From the first floor we were able to wheel the grisly cargo out into the rear parking lot. A warehouse was beyond the lot, an out-of-business restaurant across the street, a dead auto shop next door. Covid hit everybody hard.

I went around front with a key fob I'd retrieved from the bartender's soggy corpse and used it to identify and unlock the car this pair had arrived in—an aging Chevrolet Silverado, black with BOTTOMS UP painted on the sides in white. These guys had really been discreet on their killing mission, starting with Freddy the bartender's sweatshirt. You'd almost think they were a couple of idiots.

The pick-up I drove around to the rear parking lot; we transferred the two bodies into the back. Funny thing—the bartender was heavier than Theo. Go figure. Luann rounded up a tarp for us to cover them with. I would chauffeur them and she would follow in my Olds.

"We need an area being readied for construction," I said,

"that isn't too near trees or people. Somewhere with no security on-site."

She didn't have to think long. "I know just the place. Land for a new high school. Nothing built yet."

"Perfect. I'll follow you," I said. "But pull into the first convenience store."

She didn't ask why. Just nodded.

At a Casey's, I went in and got myself a Diet Coke and Luann a coffee. Also some lighter fluid and helped myself to a few books of matches.

Most of the way we went east on Beach Boulevard, then turned north on Veteran's Avenue. It was a huge cleared fenced-off area, with a NO TRESPASSING sign, with a big opening in that fence anyway, and nothing around but a few sleeping earth-movers.

She pulled my Olds in and I followed in the Silverado. The cleared-off area was vast. We couldn't see anyone and no one could see us, not without binoculars. We might as well have been on the moon. About midpoint in the middle of this brown-dirt landscape, she stopped and got out of the pick-up. I parked well behind her and trotted over. Motioned her to stand well away. Then I leaned in and doused the front seat and everywhere up there with the lighter fluid.

Getting those two stiffs up into the cab was awkward and unpleasant, but it didn't take long with the two of us. I sent her back to my Olds to wait while I did the rest of the prep, which was mostly just making sure the windows were up tight and tossing the burning matchbook in on the bartender's lap (he was driving, in a way).

I jogged back to Luann.

"Why didn't you just shoot into the gas tank?" she asked, curious not critical.

"That's TV and movies. Cars don't catch fire that easy and they never explode."

As if proving my point, nothing much was happening up there.

"We should go," I said.

"Let's make sure it's really burning," she said.

We waited until the interior of the cab turned orange and our two callers were silhouettes again. You could hear the flames snap and see them lick.

"We should go," I repeated. "That's spreading through the firewall by now, through holes for wires and tubes. In ten minutes it'll be raging through the whole engine compartment. Even out here it'll attract attention."

She was watching the fire, not in an arsonist kind of way. But fascinated, still not going anywhere. She turned to me with a look of obvious fondness. "We work well together."

"Not bad for old folks."

Her face returned to the burning car, still just the cab mostly, though smoke was escaping out from around the edges of the hood. She looked very young in the moonlight. Brought a tear to my eye.

Or maybe it was just the smoke.

TWELVE

I stayed the night with Luann at her little house on Father Ryan Avenue. The place hadn't changed much at all, but for new appliances, a big flat screen TV, and some pricey "new" antiques. She cooked me a nice breakfast and we pledged to get together again soon, minus the mayhem. Then she drove me to the nameless used car lot, where I sold the Olds back for $300 with a ride to the airport thrown in.

I caught a flight at 11:20 that got me to Memphis by way of Atlanta four hours later. In an airport men's room, I opened my carry-on bag and changed into my Ralph Lauren suit, which Luann had spruced up with a hand steamer this morning after yesterday's activities. Along the way I snugged my nine millimeter—retrieved from my checked bag—on my right hip in a black leather waistband holster. You can buy just about anything from Amazon.

Memphis was windy and overcast, colder than Biloxi but with no snow. The taxi ride from the airport to the Climax Lounge would have taken five minutes if it hadn't been rush hour, which made it all of eight. My driver's name was Babak Ahmadi, and he said maybe six words to me, clearly disappointed he wasn't getting the twenty-bucks-plus-tip for a trip downtown. We passed rental car outlets and a golf course, then were in an area of warehouses and businesses and the occasional strip mall.

The one-and-a-half-story Climax Lounge—cement-brick painted pink, red awnings over tall dark windows—sat smack in the middle of its own patch of cement. Half of the large parking lot accommodated the strip club, the other half the Climax Shop with its own entry for adult toys, books and lingerie. The latter wasn't doing much business, but the former's lot was maybe a third full, men on their way home stopping off for a drink and an eyeful.

The sun was still up, but inside it was dark, and more than one moon was rising. I stowed my carry-on in the unattended coat check and surveyed things. This was no Bottoms Up, nor was it even Lolita's back in the day—this was your typical twenty-first century gentlemen's club: mirrored walls, brass rails, a mix of pink and purple lighting, low-slung plush pink chairs at small round black tables, the impression of elegance without any. The single stage was mid-room and large enough to handle three dancers, and two were on at the moment—a black girl, lanky, in a blonde wig and a red bikini, and a busty brunette in a black bra and g-string. The black girl was barefoot and worked a pole with athletic agility; the brunette impressed only because her clear-plastic stilettos were nosebleed high, plus she had more tattoos than a Yakuza thug, which was not my cup of tee-tee.

The patrons, who also appeared to be Men's Wearhouse shoppers, seemed fine with the tattoos, however, and admittedly the rest of her was worth their white-collar dollars. A guy right now was showing off, stuffing a five-spot in her g-string, as if engravings of Abe Lincoln were still a big deal.

The only thing about this club that said Memphis or reflected the right-wing turn their namesake magazine had taken, after years of left-wing rant from their female then-editor/publisher, was the country music being strutted to. Right now "Tangled Up" by Billy Currington was segueing into "Ladies Love Country Boys" by Trace Adkins. These capitalist patrons were about as country as a country club, but they were as horny as any hick. Me, I like country music just a little less than I go for tattoos.

The bartender came over as I helped myself to a stool. She was a pretty college-age girl in the kind of bustier a guy used to be lucky to get his wife into on their honeymoon. Maybe that still took luck.

I ordered a Diet Coke with lime and asked if Mr. Climer, Mr. Montgomery Climer, was in. She said he was, but that he rarely visited the floor. That sounded like a euphemistic description for a drunk who knew when to quit. I asked if she would convey word to Mr. Climer that Ms. Breedlove's co-author would like a few minutes with him.

"Ms. Breedlove?" she asked. Her voice was a pleasant if practiced chirp.

"Yes. Susan Breedlove, the writer. She interviewed him recently. I'm her father—Jack Breedlove. Tell him it's just a brief follow-up, if he'd be so kind."

She nodded, smiled, and called a waitress over—another blonde and in the same kind of black bustier. The second blonde, not counting the black dancer, headed toward a door marked NO ADMITTANCE and admitted herself. She was in there only a few minutes, but she did not, as I expected, return to the bar with a response.

Instead, a burly mustached Hispanic in a gray suit with a black shirt came through that door and looked toward the bar, maybe at me. Then he seemed to be heading my way.

I wasn't wrong.

He planted himself before me like a tree you wouldn't dare climb and watered at your risk. There was a pause, as if I were expected to speak first, but I had nothing to say to him, so finally he spoke: "You wanted to see Mr. Climer."

It wasn't exactly a question.

"I still do," I said, and that wasn't exactly an answer.

He thought about it. I could see him trying to decide if I was being obtuse or a smartass or maybe an obtuse smartass. Possibly his thoughts didn't include the word "obtuse" at all. He might have been considering tossing my smart ass out the door.

But instead he nodded and began to walk in the direction of NO ADMITTANCE. I took this to mean I was to follow him and I did. The same two strippers were still dancing, their breasts bare now but for pasties—in Memphis, if a female wasn't nursing, she needed to keep her nipples to herself, and bottomless applied only to soft drinks and coffee. Trace Adkins was still singing. It might have been a different song, but how could anybody tell?

Going through the NO ADMITTANCE portal took us to a pink hallway where a door marked DRESSING ROOM was to the left and another marked PRIVATE was to the right. My mustached escort led me there but stood and blocked it, shaking his head.

"Gotta pat you down," he said.

"I have a gun on my hip," I informed him. Not that it was a surprise; the off-the-rack Lauren didn't hide that fact at all well.

He frowned. "Why do you?"

I shrugged. "I thought you folks liked guns in Tennessee. Concealed carry is legal here, isn't it?"

"Not in Mr. Climer's office," he said, and held out his hand.

I daintily got the nine mil out from under my coat, removed the magazine, dropped that in my suitcoat pocket, and handed the empty gun over.

"Fair enough?" I asked.

He thought about it, then nodded. He opened the door for himself, not me, and left me out there to stare at the word

PRIVATE. I heard brief, muffled talk, and then the mustached guard at the gate returned and held the door open for me. I went in and the door closed behind me a little louder than necessary. Sometimes I make a better impression than other times.

Without getting up from behind a big mahogany desk, Montgomery Climer served up a big toothy grin in his frying pan of a face. One of those strange characters whose head belongs to a fat man and whose body belongs to a skinny one, he was wearing a navy-blue tailored suit—no off-the-rack for him—with, I swear to God, a hot pink shirt and no tie. With that Elvis hair he might have been singlehandedly keeping the Vitalis company afloat; his tan was like stained furniture, and his eyes were that dark brown that reads black, with a nose dropping straight to a bulb decorated by enlarged pores. He was absolutely the kind of man who would have to run a strip club to get laid.

And he owned six.

Montgomery Climer's office was, like so much of his club, pink with touches of purple by way of plump leather chairs and an overstuffed couch in a ten-by-ten room. The space also accommodated a glass coffee table and a small conference area where back issues of *Climax* magazine were fanned out with pride. Framed oversize blow-ups of covers, lighted from behind, lined the walls, gorgeous near-naked girls literally glowing.

The exception was the wall behind the desk where a pair of black file cabinets faced each other—the space above given over to a big framed color photograph of the magazine's founder, Max Climer, with an arm around his cousin Vernon on one side and his cousin Montgomery on the other, much younger than the version I was encountering.

"So you're the Breedlove girl's father," the surviving Climer said, finally half-rising, offering a hand for me to shake, which I dutifully did. It was moist.

I settled into the comfy visitor's chair. "That is a fact, Mr. Climer."

"Call me Monty."

"And I'm Jack."

"Can I get you somethin' from the bar?" my host asked in his friendly, Southern-tinged baritone. He had a cup of coffee going on his desk, which had a few neat stacks of paper on its top and a cell phone in a charger.

"No, I'm fine, thank you."

My new pal Monty had a friendliness born of thinking he might get some good publicity out of this. "So it's like father, like daughter, then? You're a journalist too?"

"No." I half-smiled, shrugged. "Well, I worked for a magazine publisher for a while."

His eyebrows, which were on the shaggy side, shot up. "No kidding. Small world."

"Smaller than you think." I nodded toward the picture looming over him. "Back in the early '80s, I worked for your uncle."

Reflexively, Monty glanced back at the picture, as he'd forgotten it was there. "Is that right? In what capacity?"

"A kind of bodyguard."

"Really?" His manner changed. He stiffened and his pleasant expression hardened without going entirely away.

"Of course, I wasn't working for Max," I said, "at the time of his death...or should I say assassination."

"Fuckin' religious kook. Least they shot that little Lee Harvey Asshole to shit." He sneered at the memory, shook his head. "My uncle was a great man. A visionary. What a terrible loss. Then his daughter took everything he built and tore it down brick by brick and just ran it into the fuckin' ground with her leftie nonsense and feminist propaganda."

I smiled, put my right ankle on my left knee. "Maybe so, Monty, but that gave you the opportunity of a lifetime. You went from running one minor strip joint here in Memphis… the Titta Cocka Club, wasn't it?…into a newly rebuilt Climax Lounge empire."

He might have felt insulted, but appeared complimented, and swathed himself in false modesty. "It's not an empire, Jack, not really. Might be hard to believe, but I run the whole shootin' match from this desk right here…and *here*." He tapped his right temple. "We're a franchise operation, like McDonald's. This is the only club of the chain that I own and operate."

"What about the magazine?"

He gestured vaguely. "The editorial offices are downtown, where I keep another, bigger office. But I'm not in more than a day or two a week. I don't do anything except hire good people and stay the fuck out of their hair."

I put some embarrassment in my grin. "I've never been in a Climax Lounge before…well, except for the original one on the Highland Strip, which was nothing so posh—not at all what I expected."

That seemed to offend him a little. "Is that right? What *were* you expectin'?"

I shrugged. "Well, I know the magazine. I'm a subscriber." Of course my subscription lapsed thirty-some years ago. "And with the right-wing, redneck slant you brought to it…if you'll forgive that characterization…"

Monty raised a hand high, palm out. "No, Jack, you are right on the money. Those 'redneck' readers are my bread and butter."

"Well, I expected Confederate flags and MAGA hats and lots

of red, white and blue, and the closest your club comes is some country music."

He chuckled. "You mind if I smoke, Jack? It's not legal but I do own the joint."

"Be my guest."

He got a pack of Marlboros from somewhere, the way Bugs Bunny does a carrot or a machine gun, and lighted up with a Climax lighter. "My secret? My readers support me. We're the strongest survivor out there. *Penthouse* is coughin' up blood, and *Playboy* is deader than disco. Our newsstand sales dropped some during the pandemic, but our subscriptions soared. But there's a couple of subtle factors goin' here."

"Subtle?"

Monty nodded, exhaling smoke, and the Elvis hair disassembled a shade. "Those men in their suits out there? They are the ones who can pay the twenty-five buck cover, and who pony up the VIP dough for certain privileges, which we won't go into. My truck-driver, farmer, prison inmate, blue-collar and flat-out out-of-work readers love their traditional split-beaver shots seasoned with patriotic editorial content. But they can't afford to stuff foldin' money in some cutie's garter belt. Or the price of drinks or what have you. And here's the real secret—plenty of those suit-and-tie boys out there are no more liberal than the rednecks. They just don't advertise it. I sell the USA and good-old-fashioned porn, two surefire products. It's as American as pussy pie."

"Are you on the record about this?"

"Oh, I've given interview after interview on the subject. But your daughter didn't go down that road at all. She's a true-crime gal, right? Of course, you're a journalist, too, Jack. Maybe you got another market for what your daughter isn't interested in. Any publicity is good publicity, my Uncle Max used to say."

"Actually, Monty, I'm not a journalist."

"Oh? What are you, then?"

"An author."

"Would I have heard of anything of yours?"

Not "read" anything—"heard of."

I said, "Maybe a book I did, a thriller, loosely based on your late uncle's experiences here in Memphis."

Monty stared at me, his smile frozen for a while and then thawing into a scowl, but a scowl with some fear in it.

"You...you're *him*, aren't you?"

"You'll have to be more specific."

His eyes got big and he pointed at me, like Scrooge at the ghost of Christmas past. "You...my brother *Vernon*...you're the one who ki—ki—"

I held up a traffic-cop hand. "Let me explain something. That book, if you read it, or even if somebody just told you about it, was highly fictionalized. Loosely based on events here in Memphis, back in '75. If you have the idea I had something to do with your brother's tragic demise, you're quite mistaken."

He was working at staying cool but I could see he was trembling; he'd forgotten the cigarette in his fingers and a long ash was forming. "Why...why would you come here and tell me this? You could have called me. Written me. Or done nothin' at all! Why are you here?"

To kill him, he no doubt thought. But I wouldn't. Necessarily.

"Monty, a few days ago," I said, "someone tried to kill *me*."

"I don't even know where you live! You're not local!"

"No, I'm not local."

He was sitting back in his chair, like he hoped to crawl into the wall. "Well, I can *prove* I haven't been out of Memphis, not since Covid hit!"

"I believe you."

"Then why—"

"Someone hired it done."

He straightened. "*I* didn't! I wouldn't even know *how* to do such a thing. Look, I'm a businessman. A respectable businessman runnin' a respectable club. My girls are single moms and college-debt coeds. They don't hook. They keep their bottoms on and their pasties, too."

"You're just following the ordinance around here."

His chin came up and his eyes looked down, indignantly. "That's the rule at *all* of my clubs! It's part of the franchise agreement!" As if this had fuck-all to do with anything.

"If I had caused your brother's death," I said, "I could well understand you wanting to even the score."

His head jerked back. "Why would I want to do that?"

Now he had me.

"Because," I said carefully, "he was your brother."

His mouth smiled in the midst of a clenched fist of a face. "My brother was a son of a bitch and a prick. He belittled me and he fucked my uncle's wife and he stole money and, Christ, if I'd had the balls back then, *I'd've* killed his ass."

I was studying him like he was a microbe on a slide. "Really. And yet, he's right there looking over your shoulder, smiling down on you."

Monty tossed a dismissive wave over his shoulder. "*Fuck* him!" Then he leaned forward. "Look, the official story, the party line, is all three of us was peas in a pod. We conceived the magazine together and Max was the creative genius and Vernon the financial whiz and I was the artistic director."

"Weren't you?"

He sank the cigarette into his forgotten coffee with a sizzle. "Hell no! I couldn't artistically direct a fart in the bathtub! That's, what do you call it, revisionist history. I worked in the original Climax Lounge when I was just eighteen, helping book the strippers. I was management and it got me more tail than Sinatra, and probably more strains of VD, too. I didn't get smart till I got older—till I got tired of seein' Cordelia Climer flush my uncle's gold-plated dream down the shitter!"

Neither of us said anything for a while.

"What I'm telling you," I said finally, feeling a little over-whelmed by this surprising turn, "is that you shouldn't view that book I wrote as gospel."

Now I received a dismissive wave. "Fuck, I don't view the Gospel as gospel. If you killed my brother, I'd like to shake your hand. If you didn't, I'm glad *somebody* did, whether that fire he burned up in was thanks to God or you or just a random fuck-up."

He stood.

Reflexively, I did the same.

He said, "Do you figure we have any more business?"

My eyebrows went up. "I hope we don't. But if you're playing me, Mr. Climer, I'll—"

He grinned. "You'll what? Kill me? But you told me yourself, Breedlove. That book of yours was the bunk! Total bullshit! We got no problem, you and me. Now, where my niece Corrie's concerned, that might be a whole other deal."

"Oh?"

"Hell yes. That's her *father* we're talking about, after all, the late otherwise unlamented Vernon Climer. And, my friend... *she* read your book, too."

THIRTEEN

The high-income suburb of Germantown, just east of Memphis, seemed little changed. I traveled by Uber and caught glimpses of the same public parks and safe prosperous neighborhoods as forty years ago. On Scarlet Road, I was deposited at the former home of Maxwell Climer, editor and publisher of *Climax* magazine.

What had been a freshly built, near-mansion ranch-style, with its single, white-brick story, black trim, and square windows, did not betray its age. It lined up with my memory almost exactly, despite whatever paint jobs and roof repairs had been required over the years, though when I walked up the circular brick drive I found the *Climax* creator's outrageous pink door was now a tasteful black one with brass fittings.

After retrieving my carry-on bag from the strip club coat check, and calling for an Uber, I'd tried Cordelia Sundbloom's number—actually, her husband Douglas Sundbloom's number—while waiting outside for my ride. My computer savvy daughter had retrieved that number for me back at Miss Mamie's in the QC before dropping me off at the airport.

Thanks to Susan, I knew also that the unlikely female editor/publisher of the notorious *Climax* magazine had married a prominent attorney thirty-some years ago; they had a grown son and daughter and four grandchildren. She was active in community organizations and charities, including the Boys & Girls Clubs, the St. Jude Children's Research Hospital, and Let's Innovate for Education (on which she was a board member). Photos showed an attractive, respectable-looking woman in her late sixties.

I got the answering machine. "Corrie, this is an old friend who finds himself in town and wonders if there's any chance I could stop by and—"

"*Jack?*"

She had known me as Jack Quarry. That she had recognized my voice was clear by how shocked she sounded with that single word. But I was startled, too, because her voice was immediately familiar. Forty years later and the big brown eyes and hair to her shoulders and those pert breasts and that lovely bottom were all right there in my memory.

And on the phone.

"I know," I said quietly, "I'm a voice from the past and probably not a welcome one. But I need to talk to you. I don't want to embarrass you with your husband or cause any trouble. But there's something important we need to discuss."

"My husband's about to leave," she whispered, "for an evening with my daughter's two boys. He'll be out the door in fifteen minutes."

"I'm half an hour away."

"Perfect."

She rang off.

I looked at the cell phone in my palm. It could do a lot of things, that phone; but explain why a woman I hadn't seen for decades was reacting to me like I was her lover waiting for the coast-is-clear? There was no app for that.

And yet, even after that weird phone call, when the Uber pulled up in front of the former Max Climer home, I was surprised again. When Susan gave it to me, the address hadn't rung a bell—I remembered Germantown, of course, but not in this context.

But in a way it made sense: Cordelia Sundbloom's father, Vernon, and her uncle Max, both were dead. Her uncle and his late wife, Mavis, had been childless, so...who else was there to inherit the Memphis version of the Playboy Mansion but Cordelia Climer?

I rang the bell and she answered quickly, as if she'd been hanging around near the front door waiting for a pizza.

"Jack," she said through an open O of a mouth in a beautifully made-up face, accomplished with a lighter touch than many women her age. She stood poised there for a moment, looking more like fifty than almost seventy, her hair a mix of brown and silver in a fetching pixie cut, her big brown eyes wide.

Though a tad heavier than Luann, and tanned in a way the sun hadn't played much if any part in, Corrie Climer Sundbloom had retained her figure nicely. She was generously curvy in a light-blue mannish shirt with a long gold chain necklace open at a throat taut with skillful plastic surgery; her brown-belted white linen pants brushed her sandals, the red of her toenails matching her fingernails and pretty mouth. And if the pert breasts of her youth had been replaced by full matronly ones, I was not about to file any complaints.

"Corrie," I said, and there was an awkward moment—hug, kiss on the cheek, handshake...what?

The answer was...nothing, just restrained smiles and her stepping aside to hold open the door for me.

Unlike the exterior, the place had been completely done over inside, the Max Climer-dictated tacky Oil-Sheik-in-Beverly-Hills look banished. The modest entryway opened into a spacious living room where cream-color walls were tastefully hung with framed landscapes and family photos, while shelving displayed vaguely rustic knickknacks in the context of elegant yet lived-in furnishings—comfy sofas and overstuffed arm-chairs sporting upholstery in shades of brown on parquet floors.

That was in front of me and to my left. But she ushered me to the right down a little hall and into a room utterly unsuited to the rest of the place. This was apparently the only largely untouched space since the Max Climer days—that third-rate Hefner's legendary wood-paneled den with a padded bar and a massive curving sectional couch that surrounded a low-slung barge of a coffee table cushion-edged for extended seating. The only difference was Max's framed photos of his *Climax* centerfolds had been replaced by framed album covers of Memphis rock legends—Elvis, B.B. King, Johnny Cash, Carl Perkins, Booker T, among others—and a fat retro old-fashioned stand-up jukebox squatted regally in a corner.

"This is the one room," Corrie said, her smile more easy now, though mingling amusement and embarrassment, "we couldn't bring ourselves to remodel....Have you eaten? I have some lasagna in the fridge."

"No, I just ate," I lied. "Thank you, though."

"Something to drink?"

"No, I'm fine."

She gestured for me to sit at one end of the couch, where a space between sections allowed her sit next to me but not right by me.

"You know," I said, trying to make it friendly and not flirty, "you really look stunning."

She liked hearing that. Any woman who says she wouldn't is a damn liar. Any woman over forty making that claim is a god-damn liar.

She said, "You look young for your age, Jack. Really nicely..."

"Preserved? It's this boyish mug of mine."

She laughed lightly, then her expression grew serious.

"I'm sorry," she said, and folded her hands in her lap, "that I couldn't ask you over or…have you meet Doug. My husband, Doug? I'm afraid he doesn't have much patience for anyone from the early days of the magazine."

"Why is that?"

Her shrug sent her shoulders up high and they froze there for a moment before settling back down. "Doug's not stuffy, but his world is conservative…not politically as much as… socially. He was my attorney at *Climax*, that's how we met, and he respected what I did editorially, as far as the left-leaning content was concerned. He's very progressive, in his way. But ultimately the men's magazine, raunchy side of things became… a problem."

"You mean an embarrassment?"

The pixie cut bounced as she nodded. "That's why I eventually walked away from it, though admittedly our readership was declining."

Tricky combining feminism and female nudity. Her odd mix had its moment, and attracted attention, but faded.

"Your Uncle Montgomery," I said, "came along at just the right time."

Her eyebrows lifted and took their time coming down. "Yes. His swing to the right, and back to more explicit photo layouts, saved the magazine. No denying that. He's a fairly horrid man, my uncle, but a marketing genius, and, you know, the money from *Climax* continues to roll in."

"And that income *doesn't* embarrass your husband, I'm guessing."

A half-smile. "No. Not when it paid for our kids' college and bought us an Aspen time share, among other things. But, uh… Doug was there when things fell apart for me. And not just with the magazine's spiraling circulation. Cocaine addiction was the *big* problem for me, in the '80s."

"Not uncommon."

"Doug was there and he helped me through that." She looked at her hands in her lap. Sighed. "I was lucky to survive it."

"That was after my time," I said. "You were just a cute coed when I knew you."

"Blowing you in the balcony at *Rocky Horror*," she said, smiling, the words coming without thinking.

We both smiled and laughed, nervously at first, but then... just laughed. Coming from a beautiful if rather proper older female, those words had startled both of us.

Nonetheless, she returned at once to her slightly uptight demeanor. "There's another reason why I'd rather keep you and Doug in...separate compartments of my life."

"Oh? I can't imagine I'm the *only* other man in your past."

She chuckled, and the big brown eyes settled warmly on me. "Funny thing is, Jack. We never did *do* it...other than a, uh..."

"Blow job? In the balcony?"

She nodded, embarrassed but amused. "I was in my period. Otherwise..."

"A woman never has to apologize to a man about a blow job."

"If her husband finds out she does."

"How would he find out?"

She gave me an unblinking look, the big brown eyes huge now, eyebrows climbing halfway up her forehead. "*Really*, Jack?"

"...Oh."

My book. The one she'd been in.

"Listen, about that," I said. The grin I gave her would best be described as shit-eating. "You need to know something. That was highly fictionalized. I was just riffing on some things that happened to me, and happened *around* me, and I turned it into a good story. I hope, a good story."

She'd started shaking her head halfway through that. "You don't have to say that."

But I did. Because I killed her father. I set a fire. Norwegian wood. Isn't it good.

"My anti-hero killed the character based on your father," I said. "That doesn't mean *I* did it."

She reached across the divide between couch sections and put her hand on mine. Her warm hand. "Listen to me, Jack. You don't have to say that."

"I'm...I'm not following."

Her eyes weren't wide. "I wasn't close to my father. You know that. He was a terrible man. A cheater. A thief. *Himself* a murderer, based upon all reliable evidence. If it got him killed, that's on him. If you are the guy in the book, that's on you, and your conscience. Assuming you have one."

That was a whole other discussion.

She went on: "I don't think you came looking for me to try to convince me you didn't do what the character in your book did. I mean, it was published several years ago, and you didn't come around then. But *Doug* read it, and boy did I have to do some fancy talking."

"I hope you told him all of that sex stuff wasn't real, even if that character seemed to be based on you."

Her chin came up. "Oh, I *told* him that all right. That it was a bunch of baloney. Only, Jack, I knew it was real, because everything you wrote about the two of us was exactly the way it happened."

And she was sending me a sort of signal: she knew damn well I had killed her father. Burned him and his lover to death and neither my conscience nor I gave a fuck.

Her eyes were tight now, studying me. "So why are you *really* here, Jack?"

I told her, and I was frank about it. I said I had indeed spent five years post-Vietnam as a contract killer. Did not deny that at all. And maybe she'd read that book, and perhaps some or all of my other ones, because she just nodded and took it in, matter of fact. I did make the point that my mission in Memphis, nearly half a century ago, had not been a contract job, and that I had in fact been sent to prevent the killing of her Uncle Max, a task I succeeded at. His death sometime later at a religious zealot's hands was a separate incident.

"When you were sent here to prevent the hired killing," she said, putting the pieces together, "it was my *father* who wanted my uncle dead."

"Yes. My first stop before coming here was to talk to your *other* uncle, Monty, to determine whether he was behind what happened a few days ago."

"*What* happened a few days ago?"

I told her about the team that came around to try to kill me on my home ground.

"Oh dear!" she said.

I reported only that I'd dealt with them. She was too good a person to be burdened with such grisly details. I mean, it might make her say "Oh dear!" again.

Frowning in thought, she said, "You wondered if maybe my uncle sent them because of my father's death? For, what… revenge? Even after so much time has passed?"

I nodded.

She shook her head and her smile was not the joyful variety. "No. No way. He *hated* my father. Uncle Monty would have bought you a steak dinner and a cigar, not hired somebody to do you in."

I liked that: do you in. She was still a cute kid, even in her sixties.

"I don't think anybody from those days," she continued, "is left around here, who might cause you trouble. My uncle certainly didn't do it." She frowned, leaned forward. "Please don't kill him or anything."

I waved that off. "No, he convinced me. He's not the one."

The brown eyes got big again, fast. "You don't think *I'm* the one, do you?"

"No. Of course not."

But I had come to see her, and I hadn't been sorry to hear that her husband wouldn't be home. And my nine millimeter was back in the hip holster from Amazon. Killing her was nothing I would ever consider, not in a million years...unless she had hired the hit.

"*Somebody* sent those people after you," she said. "Who could it have been?"

"Like Hamlet says, that is the question." I shrugged a shoulder. "I had a lead in Biloxi but it went nowhere. The true-crime writer I'm working with..." I had not revealed to Corrie that Susan was my daughter. "...has been researching another lead back in the Midwest. That's where I'll be heading now."

She glanced at her watch. We'd only been talking half an hour.

Then she said, "You know what else we didn't mess with in the house?"

"No. What?"

"That crazy hot tub of Uncle Max's."

I chuckled. "No kidding."

Her head bobbed up and down, all that cute silver and brown hair. "And, uh, well...you know, Doug won't be home for hours and hours. They're taking in a movie, after Chuck E. Cheese, and he has to take them back to Arlington."

I thanked her but said no. What was this, the geriatric sex tour? But I kissed her on the cheek before I left.

The question is…what cheek?

FOURTEEN

An early flight the next morning routed me through Chicago and got me back to Moline by early afternoon. Susan—her black puffy parka unzipped, furry hood back to reveal nicely tousled light-blonde hair—met me at the airport. In an orange cashmere turtleneck sweater and black velvet jeans, she looked younger than any woman well into her forties had any right. I was back in the Ralph Lauren, which the Memphis Quality Inn's laundry service had given a new lease on life. We looked like a respectable older businessman meeting a trophy wife young enough to be his daughter.

The lunch rush was over at Miss Mamie's and we were able to settle into a corner booth where we could have a leisurely meal and catch each other up. For now, I was guarded about what I shared about the Biloxi trip. I told her I had reconnected with Luann but skipped the personal part. As for Theo Brunner, I said he indeed held a grudge, but that he would not be a problem.

"Oh?" she said, between bites of her garlic salad with shrimp. "Why is that?"

I was having the crab cakes. "He, uh, passed away. Unexpectedly."

She thought about that, seemed to be about to ask a follow-up question, then had another bite of salad and shrimp instead. If she wanted to press me for details in a less public place, that was fine.

"As for the *Climax* magazine crowd," I said, after a sip of Diet Coke, "there are only two real possibilities."

She nodded. "Montgomery Climer and his niece Cordelia Sundbloom. You saw them both?"

"I did, and we can rule them out, provisionally at least."

She gave me a sideways look. "They didn't both...pass away, did they? Unexpectedly?"

"No. They're quite above ground. But neither of them had fond memories of the late Vernon Climer. His brother hated him and his daughter was ashamed to have him for a father."

She frowned. "But did they know of, or suspect, your role in his, uh...passing?"

"They did. They do."

"Yet you rule them out."

Another sip of Diet Coke—the fountain variety, with ice, my preference. "If I were a cop, I wouldn't call them suspects. Persons of interest, maybe. I believe them. Of course, people *have* been known to lie."

"At last," she said dryly. "Some fatherly advice."

"Maybe I've been on a fool's errand," I said, dipping a forked chunk of crab cake into remoulade sauce. "In my reckless younger days, I did make more than my share of enemies. How can we hope, at this late date, to zero in on just the right one?"

She breathed in, breathed out, and prepared to dig back into that salad. "We just stay at it."

I pushed my plate away, abandoning half a crab cake. "I don't think so. We're operating from the premise that your research for a sequel stirred somebody up. But my books were already out there. Anybody involved in what I wrote about could have started putting two and two together."

Susan paused. A matronly waitress stopped by to freshen her coffee and disappeared.

"Maybe so," my daughter said, "but looking hard at what I may have accidentally sparked is still your best bet."

"My best bet is to go back to Sylvan Lake, arm myself heavily, booby-trap my fucking house, then sit back and let the fuckers come at me...and deal with their asses."

"Said the old guy who will turn seventy if he's very lucky."

I leaned forward and tried for menace but didn't quite make it. "Listen. Little girl? I don't want to endanger you unnecessarily. Get me?"

She smiled and put her hand on top of mine.

"How do you know," I said, "I don't consider you a danger that needs dealing with? You may already've put an end to the comfortable life I've been living. You wrote the book about me—if you know *anything* about Quarry, you know self-preservation is the only thing that matters to him."

She did not seem impressed. "You would 'deal with' *me*?"

I removed her hand. "How do you know I wouldn't?"

She leaned forward and whispered: "Because you are not capable of killing your own daughter. Because self-preservation hasn't turned you into pure fucking evil."

"Yet," I said.

The matronly waitress stopped by for our dishes. My daughter and I looked at each other like nervous gunfighters waiting for the other to draw first. Then the waitress and our dirty dishes disappeared.

Susan sat back and sighed. She was looking at me with a frustratingly bland expression. No fear in her at all.

"We should," she said, "play out the hand we dealt ourselves."

"Meaning what?"

Her shrug couldn't have been more casual, but her words had spine in them. "We still have the Kinman path to go down. That's what I've been digging into while you were off calling on your old girlfriends."

"Arnold Kinman is dead." The Broker's right-hand man at the Concort Inn, his hotel and base of operations.

"*Jeffrey* Kinman isn't—Arnold's son by Donna, the housekeeper at the Concort who surprised everybody by being a born businesswoman. She almost single-handedly built the Mississippi Queen casino empire."

"Eight casinos, you said."

A small single nod. "Right. The flagship casino is across from the Concort, where its riverboat precursor was docked."

"Last I knew," I said, "you were having trouble getting Jeffrey Kinman to sit still for an interview."

Her eyebrows flicked up and down. "I've reached him by phone half a dozen times. He's been friendly and cooperative, but always too busy to see me just then. We had two appointments he cancelled at the last minute."

"And you haven't nailed him down in my absence?"

"No. But I've been working all my local PD and media contacts—strictly as a true-crime writer doing background research. Very discreetly. And, of course, more Internet research and even old-fashioned library visits, going through microfiche."

"And?"

Her eyes narrowed and she sat forward again, hands folded on the table, as if preparing to say grace. "There have been rumors through the years...the kind that gain a certain weight and velocity over time...linking the Kinmans to the Chicago Outfit."

I made a skeptical face. "Wouldn't that be ancient history?"

Her eyebrows went up again. "It wasn't, back in your Broker's day. And the Outfit's still a going concern, underwriting robbery crews, and wholesaling and importing cocaine and heroin. Word is a substantial share of their income comes from their shares in the casino business. Of course the Gaming Boards wouldn't allow that, which is where the late Arnold and Donna and their very much alive son, Jeffrey, come in."

The waitress dropped off a fresh Diet Coke and left.

"Okay," I said. "Fine. But whatever remains of the old bent-nose bunch has no gripe with me. Back in the day, I did jobs for them, through the Broker. And the Kinmans only benefitted from somebody 'rubbing out' the Broker…so if they think it was me, so what? I made their success possible when daddy Arnold inherited the two-percent that gave him control of the Concort."

Then, out of nowhere, she said, "Tell me about the Broker."

"Come on, you know the basics. He looked me up in a Hollywood flop house. I was drinking more than Coca-Cola then. He saw the write-up in the papers about how this re-turning Vietnam 'hero' came home to his wife fucking a guy and killed him a day later. Shit, Susan. You wrote this story yourself."

Her eyes were glittering and her smile was small. "But you *lived* it. I do know the story, only…what was he like, your Broker? What was his…deal?"

My shrug took its time. "Obviously, he liked young men. He always had a protégé with him, and he recruited in those days from that aimless army of Viet vets like me, who'd got them-selves in trouble, who couldn't find honest work…yeah, what came to be called Post-Traumatic-Stress-type casualties."

"Young men," she said, narrow-eyed. "Did he ever make anything like a…sexual advance toward you?"

"No. Never. And he treated me like I was his favorite, I was special, trusted with assignments nobody else could handle, he'd say. It was always a sort of father-and-son relationship, right up to when he tried to have me killed."

"Why would he have done that?"

My laugh was almost a wheeze. "You read the novel, right?

He put me in a position where I was handling and helping distribute smack. I'd seen what that shit had done in country, to my buddies, and was having none of it. He *knew* how I felt about that."

"Why would he have put you in that position?"

"I'd been doing jobs for five years or so. Mostly with my partner, the one Broker nicknamed Boyd. We had a few jobs go slightly south. Maybe we'd outlived our usefulness. And I did some jobs for Broker that weren't straight contract work. Similar to the kind of thing I did on my own—going in and stopping a hit by a competitor of his, that kind of thing. So maybe I knew too much. That can always get you killed."

"Was Boyd gay, like in the books?"

"Does the Pope shit in the woods? He was a good man, Boyd, till the job got to him."

She was thinking so hard it must have hurt. "And the Broker… was *he* gay? He'd recruited Boyd, hadn't he? Another vet with combat experience?"

"Yeah. But the Broker liked the ladies, as we used to say. I just figured…never mind."

"What, Jack?"

My sigh hung in the air. "You have to understand. The Broker seemed so damned straight, just to look at him. Always a suit and tie or whatever was in style. Like when hair got long, his got just long enough to look hip without alienating his country club crowd. His tiny mustache got bigger, too. It was like he walked out of a high-class liquor ad. He was your banker or insurance man, the president of the Chamber. Active in Rotary and the Elks, and just a goddamn good citizen. Who married a young woman who…nothing."

"Like in your book, Jack?" She leaned in. "Did he *really* marry his own daughter?"

"She didn't know. She didn't know."

"Unless she read your book."

I batted that away. "I couldn't say. We never had contact again. What I do know is...the Broker was, under all that slick surface, one twisted motherfucker. He would fuck anything he felt like fucking, and I mean that figuratively *and* literally."

Her eyebrows were high again, the big blue eyes narrow. "Does that tell us anything about the Kinmans? The dead husband and wife? The son, who's running things now?"

"If anything," I said, "based upon my experience? They should have hated him. The Broker fucked everyone over, eventually."

Her nod came in slow motion. "And yet he left Arnold that two-percent."

"He did. Tell me, Susan."

"Yes?"

"Does Jeffrey Kinman have an office where he keeps regular hours?"

"He does. At the hotel."

"Would he be there now?"

"Good chance he is."

"So what do you think? Cold call?"

She smiled, nodded. "Cold call."

I grabbed the check.

The Concort Inn had been given a facelift since I'd seen it last—more than likely a couple. But it was still modern-looking, in the twentieth century idea of modern anyway—a glass and blue-tinged steel ten-story slab on a block's worth of parking lot, with vertical neon streaks between floors: red, white, blue, red, white, blue, a giant, gaudy, patriotic headstone.

A many-windowed walkway from the hotel arced across River Drive to the Mississippi Queen casino, which sat on the river's concrete shore. The casino, with its own parking ramp nearby, was designed to invoke the shape of the boat it replaced. Like the hotel across the way, the massive rectangular structure wore plenty of mostly vertical red, white and blue neon, with gamblers pouring in like the animals going two by two.

Our gamble, however, would take place not in the casino, but in that all-too familiar hotel.

Susan parked her Cadillac in the front lot and I followed her into the lobby, which I didn't recognize at all, the layout switched around and the '70s-style decor long gone, currently going with the red-white-and-blue theme. We did not stop at the front desk but walked confidently to the elevators and went up to the ninth-floor offices, the tenth given over to penthouse suites.

I followed Susan's lead, as she'd been here several times before, trying to line up an interview with Kinman. The floor was a rabbit's warren of cubicles, which were empty—four P.M. being quitting time, and we were ten minutes past that. This exodus had included the reception desk, behind which a huge framed expressionistic oil painting of the original Mississippi Queen riverboat dominated a wall of wide red and white and blue metallic perpendicular stripes.

But Susan knew that Kinman always worked till at least five, not coming in till eleven. She'd found this out, on a previous visit, chatting with the receptionist behind her white-trimmed red-and-blue cube of a desk—a woman who had left at four P.M. with everybody else.

Kinman's office was, Susan knew, through and beyond the rabbit warren, out of the line of fire. Another cube of a desk sat empty and, behind it, a door merely said

MISSISSIPPI QUEEN, INC.

PRIVATE

as apparently the CEO of the company liked to maintain a low profile. If so, he should have kept his secretary on till five.

Susan walked right in and I followed. The office was not massive but it was certainly good-size. The walls were not red, white and blue, but a tasteful light brown with shades-of-brown brick behind a massive two-tone cherry desk with half a dozen neat stacks of paper and a double computer monitor; a matching cabinet snugged against a side wall. Milk chocolate couches faced each other from the side walls, which were arrayed with framed photos, and a picture window to the right looked out on the casino and the river.

I took a closer look at the photos, which had Jeffrey Kinman smiling and posing with the expected celebrities and politicians, but a good number were of his mother and himself over the years. A beautiful woman and a happy son.

A large framed photographic portrait of the distinguished-looking African-American woman at perhaps sixty, wearing a light-blue pantsuit and cream-color blouse with pearls, seated with her hands in her lap, loomed over all, including the handsome man in his forties seated at the desk.

The younger man resembled the older woman in the portrait, although her complexion was a rich mahogany and his was coffee-with-cream. He was in a dark-blue blazer with a light-blue shirt and a darker-blue tie, and the hand holding the phone bore two gold rings, the other hand a gold bracelet.

Seeing him in the flesh, he reminded me—as he had in the photo I'd seen—of what singer Sam Cooke might have looked like had he lived to middle age and not been shot in a motel: a handsome, narrow face with wide-set, sharply focused eyes and a strong jaw, his close-cropped hair salt-and-pepper, though mostly still pepper.

We took root halfway across the room, but his only reaction

was to raise a palm, then nod to two padded leather visitor chairs, as if we were expected. No anger, no irritation showed at all.

We sat dutifully as his conversation continued.

"Yes…yes, we can use them at all eight facilities. And of course we'll provide lodging and provide a generous food allowance.… Yes, thank you, Mr. Axler.…Pleasure doing business with you, too. We're thrilled to be featuring the Association at our casinos."

He clicked off and he leaned back in a high-backed chair.

"Ms. Breedlove," he said, in a melodic tenor. "I've been expecting you."

"I had no appointment."

His laugh was light and calming. "I know. What I meant was, I was expecting you to assert yourself before *too* very long, putting you off as I have been. And who is this gentleman?"

"This is my father—John Breedlove," she said, with a gesture.

I said, "Make it 'Jack.' I'm a retired journalist, giving my daughter a hand with the research. Not that she really needs any help from an old goat like me."

"It's nice to see," he said, nodding, apparently sincere. "Family is important. Business is necessary, and makes things possible for families, but it's only a means to an end."

I nodded over his shoulder. "Your mother."

"Yes. Donna Lee Kinman. Donna Lee *Jackson* Kinman. One of the most successful African-American businesswomen in the Midwest. Certainly in the Quad Cities.…Now I can only spare you perhaps fifteen minutes, so I'll stop wasting it."

"I have a few questions," Susan said, "about your late father."

Kinman leaned a casual arm on his desk. "All right. But I was in junior high when he passed. And he was a busy man, rather driven. Too driven in my opinion. I was an only child, and I admit I was closer to my mother. *She* was busy, too, yet when she stepped into my father's shoes here, when the Concort Inn was the entire business, she *still* always had time for me."

Susan was nodding. "And brought you into the business at an early age."

"She did. I worked here through high school and on, and took Business at Augustana, just as she had. There was no question where I was headed."

"You were fine with that?"

His smile was almost shy. "Oh yes. I always had a head for numbers. Pretty good at science, too."

"The man I call 'the Broker,' " she said, "in my book *Sniper*…? He was your father's business partner."

"And friend."

"Is that why he left your father controlling interest in the Concort?"

A nod. "That's my understanding. You have to understand, I never met the man…your 'Broker.' But I will say, and I don't mean to be at all confrontational, that your *Sniper* book makes him out to be something I don't believe he ever was. You *must* know, as a responsible journalist, how highly regarded he was, in his day, in the community. He was on college and charity boards. He was a huge donor to United Way, for example. Your suggestion in your book that he was some kind of…'agent' for contract killers, frankly? To me, it's absurd. And you have nothing to back that up but conjecture, a few unreliable inter-view subjects, and some cheap paperbacks fictionalizing that era in the Quad Cities."

I said, "This 'Broker' was in fact found dead in a car not far from Davenport."

He nodded. "Outside Buffalo, Iowa, near the limestone quarry there."

"A young man, a disabled Vietnam veteran, was found shot to

death in that car as well. And a body in the trunk, with his skull crushed, apparently by a wrench."

"I'm not as familiar with this," he said, "as you seem to be, Jack."

I shrugged. "I'm just saying, the two dead men found with him had criminal records. And your father's business partner had been shot to death, in their company. Doesn't it suggest my daughter's research has uncovered some very disturbing facts?"

Kinman was already shaking his head. "Not really. Ms. Breedlove's put together some theories. But the facts don't add up to anything except the tragic death of a respected pillar of the community, a businessman of stellar reputation. The thinking at the time, I understand, is that the man who you consider to be a 'Broker' of contract killers was really the victim of a kidnapping gone badly awry."

My forehead tensed. "Who kidnapped who exactly?"

His smile tightened. For the first time he seemed irritated with us. "Don't ask me. I wasn't even born yet. Now…I think the time I promised you is just about up. Is there anything else? As long as you don't intend to drag out that hoary old rumor about the Capone mob having their fingers in the legal casino business? I've heard that canard since grade school."

Susan stood and so did I.

She said, "No, I think we have what we need for now. I may approach you for a follow-up."

He grinned, the irritation fading. "You'll have to catch me first."

He half-rose and gestured toward the door. Then he nodded to us and sat back down; as we exited, we could hear him on the phone again.

In the parking lot, we sat in the Caddy and I said, "You know, the Broker was not exactly noted for having the milk of human kindness in his veins. Why would he have left that controlling two-percent to Jeffrey's daddy? Which is, after all, how the younger Kinman wound up with all this. The Broker's wife received certain properties upon his death, but not the very lucrative Concort Inn, which of course evolved into an empire, probably with Chicago's help. But it seems everybody who would know the 'why' of any of it is dead."

She didn't say anything. She was thinking.

Then she said, "Maybe not. I know someone from those days. Someone who won't talk to me, but just might to you…."

FIFTEEN

The nursing home was out Utica Road in Davenport, and I had the usual sense of dread anybody my age—hell, maybe any age —had about visiting there.

But retired *Quad Cities Times* reporter and columnist Hal Lehman resided in a "townhouse" in the clustered-together independent-living cottages on the Lutheran Manor Homes campus, which made it sound like elderly cheerleaders might be waiting just around the next corner.

The housing addition-like area was certainly less forbidding than a floor of withered souls with oxygen nosepieces and wheelchairs while bleach and cleanser worked overtime to quell the smells of urine and cafeteria food. But it didn't make me feel any better about getting older and where I might be headed.

This was another cold call, and I knew I had some fast talking to do. Susan said Lehman was furious with her for not giving him proper credit in *Sniper*, which (he said) drew heavily from his self-published *Notorious Quad Cities* book.

"Really," she told me, "I gave him generous credit and thanks in my afterword. But he made about a dollar fifty on his book and mine got in the airports, on the *New York Times* bestseller list, and on TV, and he feels he got screwed over."

"I know the feeling," I said.

I left the gray Chevy Impala, bequeathed to me by that kid back at the Sylvan Lodge fitness center, in the driveway. The little white-trimmed red-brick house with its snow-covered lawn looked like Beaver Cleaver might live next door, and the

Beav would have been old enough, too. The compound of cottages looked more like an overgrown model train village than the real thing.

I knocked and it took a while for him to answer. He was small and skinny, a fact emphasized by his yellow long-sleeve shirt, the front of which had been turned into an abstract work of art thanks to assorted unidentifiable food stains, and baggy brown pants belted just under his rib cage. His cheeks were sunken and his eyes were deep in their sockets, and his hair was thin and white and short and swept back. He looked more like a monkey than a man, and yet the eyes were sharp and the mouth had a sneer that said somebody was home. Maybe not somebody nice, but home.

And a cigarette was dangling from thin, purple lips, like a dare.

"Not buying," he said, and began to shut the door.

I stopped it with my left palm. "I'm Susan Breedlove's father. I'm here with an apology."

That creased his forehead. He already knew I was stronger than he was and had given up on any upright Indian wrestling match with that door.

Then the forehead smoothed as much as possible and his chin came up. "About fuckin' time. But it's your *girl* who should be saying she's sorry."

"It's cold," I said, "and I don't have a topcoat."

I was still in the Ralph Lauren.

"Is that my fault?" he asked, not unreasonably.

"No, but let me in so we can come to agreeable terms."

That creased the forehead again. He nodded and let me in.

The two-bedroom mini-ranch-style—you could have put twelve of them in Corrie Sundbloom's place—was obviously a nice example of independent living on a nursing home campus. It had a living room and a kitchen and that driveway led to a one-car garage; a glimpse of hallway indicated two bedrooms, opposite each other, and at the end a bathroom door, ajar on a walk-in tub. Big windows looked out on a patio and a white back yard with ice-coated trees beyond. The furnishings were new yet old-fashioned. As a waiting room to the boneyard, it was hard to beat.

But my wizened host had decorated the place in a very personal style. Newspapers and magazines and books, none looking new, were stacked and tossed and even flung here and there. Ashtrays brimmed. Beer cans loitered. A small flat-screen rode a wall, like a window on the future, and some framed articles and journalism awards hung haphazardly. The kitchen that the little living room opened onto had a full sink of dirty dishes and counters cluttered with assorted carry-out boxes. You couldn't have paid me to look in his refrigerator.

Lehman went over and cleared a patch of couch and I sat. Using a kitchen match, he lighted himself another Camel—a mostly used pack was on a coffee table with Leonard Maltin movie guides and a battered copy of *Notorious Quad Cities*. Then, after I'd declined his offer of a smoke, he sat down in a faux-leather brown recliner that was the only such space that didn't require clearing before seating.

"I didn't think," I said, "you could smoke in a nursing home."

"This isn't a nursing home. It's a private residence. And you can smoke wherever the hell you want in Iowa, if it isn't public. This is still fucking *America*, last time I looked!"

He noticed me taking in the surroundings.

"If the mess bothers you," he said, "you know where the door is."

"Not at all. You should see my place."

At least it didn't smell like bleach or cleanser or even smoke in here. Pine tree spray, I'd say. A lot of it.

"My wife died six months ago," he said, as if that explained it, then added, "She was a neat freak. Since then, I live how I want. Gets a tad out of hand, after while, I guess."

"You must pay a pretty penny here," I said. "You'd think they'd throw in housekeeping services."

"Oh they do. Once a week."

I couldn't bring myself to ask if they'd already been by this week.

I said, "I'm helping my daughter on her follow-up book. And Susan wants you to know she intends to make up for the disservice she paid you on her previous effort."

"She *plagiarized* me, you know!"

She hadn't, of course. She had merely quoted and paraphrased his non-fiction work.

But I said, "Let's put the past behind us. Any material from your book that she uses, this time around, she will pay for. Any help you give us on this new project, she will credit in full."

He thought about that. Sucked in some tobacco smoke to see what the remainder of his lungs might do with it. Then he began to slowly nod.

"That's more like it, that's more like it. *That*…is more like it."

"Good," I said. "If you don't mind, I'd like to get started—ask you a few questions."

"Under this new arrangement, you bet." He was cheerful now. A whole new breed of monkey. "How about a beer?"

That would require a withdrawal from his refrigerator. But a can or bottle should be safe. So I said sure.

He got up and returned with a can of Pabst Blue Ribbon for me and for himself. I have to admit that I wasn't even sure they still made that shit.

Wasn't bad, though.

"We're focusing on the man Susan refers to," I said, "as 'the Broker.' "

Lehman nodded, and snorted, and uttered the Broker's real name as if it were an expletive.

"Around here, they thought he was a regular pillar of society. I don't know if he was a 'broker' of contract killings like your daughter claims...though since his death, that theory has gained some traction, short of any real facts to back it up."

"That's the theory we're exploring. I'm especially interested in the Broker's business relationship with Arnold Kinman, and assertions that Kinman and his wife and now his son, Jeffrey, are fronting for Chicago mob interests in the legal casino business."

He gestured with a Camel-in-hand. "It's more than a rumor. I had death threats and even got throttled once, when I ran stories to that effect, oh, twenty-five years ago. I smelled mob all over those murders at the quarry outside Buffalo, for example —that's where your Broker got himself killed, you know."

"Is that right?"

He made a face, which with that wrinkled mug was really something. "And he was one big *phony*, your Broker. Kinman's wife, Donna? She was smart, oh Christ was she smart...but a barracuda. All smiles, sharp as hell, but behind those butter-wouldn't-melt manners, tougher and meaner than any man. And her *son* is the same, though I've never been able to prove it. I interviewed him half a dozen times, asking all the tough questions...but all I got was smiles and fluff."

"My daughter and I talked to him this afternoon. We didn't get much of anything out of him, either."

"And you won't!" Lehman grunted a laugh. "He still got that wall of pictures?"

"He does."

Within the sunken sockets, the eyes narrowed. "See how many of those photos are of him and his mama, over time?"

"I noticed."

"How many pictures of him and his old man d'you see?"

I shook my head. "Not any. Might've missed some. Of course, Arnold Kinman died when Jeffrey was just in junior high, didn't he?"

Stained-yellow choppers emerged from thin purple lips to blast a big smile. "Okay, so how many pictures of them together at *any* age did you see?"

"None."

Lehman cackled. "You wanna know the best-kept secret in this whole shootin' match? That Broker of yours had a real special kink—if it was forbidden, he wanted it. That smooth, bright surface hid something dark and twisted. Start with this: Arnold Kinman was gayer than Rock Hudson and Liberace put together...and the Broker had a *thing* for him."

I shrugged. "I always suspected Broker was bisexual."

"*Bisexual!* Fuck, *omni*-sexual. Arnold was kept boy, for years and years, even after the Broker's pretty young wife come along ....But Donna—back when such things just weren't done—she was his colored girl on the side. You should've seen what she looked like, when she was working at the Concort. Made Lena Horne look like Moms Mabley!"

"So Arnold was the Broker's beard? And Donna's *for* the Broker?"

The little monkey man nodded. "I had a reliable source tell me Donna was going to expose her sugar daddy if he didn't 'treat her right.' He did that by marrying her off to Arnold and building up her new husband's interests in the hotel and, eventually, putting control in his will. So Donna would benefit. And all the while...he was bangin' 'em both. Each thinking they were the special one. What a nasty, horny, phony piece of work he was."

"You knew this and never got it into print?"

He shook his head and his expression conveyed fathomless

contempt, some of it likely for himself. "The *Times* wanted nothing to do with it. This so-called Broker was a big man in this town. And it's a sweet slice of irony, isn't it, that his colored-gal squeeze took over his place as a power broker in this very white town....Another Pabst, Breedlove?"

When I left the nursing home campus, dusk had fallen, but by the time I was crawling along East River Drive, almost to Susan's, rush hour had turned a ten- or fifteen-minute drive into a fifteen- or twenty-five-minute one, and night had taken over.

Slowing the Impala, I neared the mouth of the driveway, my turn signal on, when a car burst out of there in front of me, a dark red Dodge Charger, recent model. I had to slam on the brakes and cars behind me honked, and I started to swear but it stuck in my throat.

I'd caught a glimpse of the driver, and he wasn't pretty—an oblong-headed broad-shouldered guy with short black hair standing up, a scar on his high forehead, and a jutting fuck-you jaw. In a black sports jersey, maybe thirty, white, muscular. His rider was white, too, a heavy-set guy with glasses and short brown hair and a fat neck that rose to a fat face with only a small chin sticking out to differentiate. Another guy was in back, on the rider's side, but I couldn't really see much of him. What I could see—in the second and a half I had to take all this in—was a frightened woman's face in the window behind the driver.

Susan.

And she had seen me, but I knew she wouldn't tip that. Somehow in that fraction of a second she'd realized I'd seen this and would do something about it and the last thing she'd ever do was let the assholes who grabbed her know that I was on to them.

Up ahead the Charger's tail said ILLINOIS above, DABEARZ between, and LAND OF LINCOLN below in a CHICAGO license plate frame. Probably not a big leap to figure these guys were Outfit.

As we tooled along East River Drive, mansions on the right, parks and construction and boathouses on the left, I slipped out of the suitcoat for easier access to the nine mil on my hip. Got out of the necktie just to get out of it. The four-lane thoroughfare made it easier for me to keep a few cars between me and the Charger, yet still maintain the tail without much trouble. They weren't speeding, after all—in fact were staying right at the limit and not the safe five miles over.

I followed them under the government bridge and past downtown Davenport and then west through the city's outskirts on Highway 61. They drove steadily, attracting no attention, and I had enough traffic to stay undetected, or at least I hoped so.

At some point, I put the nine mil on the seat next to me. I was having to work at staying relaxed, thrown by how this threat to my daughter's life was working on me. My heart was pounding and I was definitely losing my cool, hands on the wheel clenching and unclenching and clenching again, and I would stop that for a while, and then I'd be doing it again.

Davenport was almost a memory when the red Charger veered off to catch Highway 22—the River Road. With the lights of the city behind us, the dark of night really kicked in, but with a rising full moon working against it. Soon, the buildings of the limestone quarry rose like a gray sooty dystopian city in the aftermath of a nuclear war, rusted-out silos, scaffolding, featureless square and rectangular buildings, smokestacks, enclosed conveyor belts crossing the under-highway, rumbling as they went.

That was the river side of the road. On the other side yawned the deep massive abyss with its tiers of gray/white rock, an end-less ugly, beautiful parody of the Grand Canyon where nature was banished and only dust and a man-made crater remained.

Work was still going on here, but mostly underground. The surface itself had been played out and what remained was largely a vast, craggy nothingness, a skeleton picked clean by predators. I was alone on the highway behind the Charger now, but keeping some distance, which was the best I could do—traffic here was minimal, the little town ahead, Buffalo, home to maybe a thousand, many at work here. Underground.

Aboveground, nothing.

Then the Charger turned right onto one of many work lanes, this one at the far end of the chasm, away from the chalky city of minarets and mausoleums. I followed, cutting my lights, having to take it slow as, even at a modest speed, they'd left me a dust cloud to navigate. No work lights up here, either, with only the moon to tell me we were driving along the edge of the kind of drop-off where you could run out of scream before hit-ting literal rock bottom.

But the dust cloud dissipated. I slowed as, about a football field away, the Impala approached a typically desolate area where a low-slung trailer-like portable building had been plopped down. Its facade had doors at far left and far right, each with a few steps up to a small landing. The structure had a battered look, like something left behind in a war. To the near end of it and back a ways lurked heavy machinery—backhoe, dump truck, excavator, bulldozer, lined up like dinosaurs waiting for the comet to come kill them.

The Charger was pulling up to the portable building and I swung behind an eight-foot mound of gravel and got out, nine mil in hand, leaving the motor running. I came around to where I could see what was going on.

They had parked vertically in front of the portable building. The guy with an oblong head and a taller guy I didn't know were hauling Susan, still in her orange sweater, up the steps to the far door. She wasn't cooperating, squirming, kicking, fighting. Wearing black Chicago Bulls hoodies, they had her by either arm with pistols in their free hands, and the oblong-headed guy was swearing at her, telling her to settle down or get the fuck killed.

The fat one with glasses and a neck-head was nowhere in sight. Maybe he'd already gone in—a light was on. The two in Bulls hoodies dragged a still uncooperative Susan inside and shut the door behind them.

I considered approaching on foot, but figured it better to have the Impala running and waiting and handy, in case I decided to go in there and grab her and shoot people and make some kind of getaway. It was less than a plan, but I returned to the car, snugged the nine mil back on my hip, and guided the vehicle slowly, trying not to make any more noise than necessary, rock crunching under me, and began crossing the football field-like distance.

About halfway there, a motor filled the night with its low rumbling growl, like a big beast waking. I turned and two bright lights, giant headlights, blinded me and that motor grew louder as huge wheels crushed gravel as speed increased and lights got ever larger as the vehicle came closer. With it bearing down on me, I started scrambling toward the rider-side door.

But then it was on me, and the bulldozer's big steel bucket nudged the driver's side and pushed, and pushed, and pushed, and then the Impala was going over the edge sideways, falling, scraping on rock as it went, tires trying to find purchase in the air while I got tossed around within.

With a *whump* the Impala hit a ledge, on its passenger side, and I could feel the vehicle teetering. I scrambled back to the driver's seat, hoping I could climb out, and that the door still worked, that the dozer bucket had pushed but not crushed, and, yes, it opened, and I crawled out and across the vehicle toward its trunk, even as it tottered like a drunk on a tightrope, and I hopped onto the ledge behind the wobbling car and landed on my side just as it went over, metal scraping rock, whining in protest, the car bouncing off the ledges below and landing hard.

I looked down and it had hit on one end and now was just a ragged mass of metal, a paper cup crushed in a giant's hand. I could hear the bulldozer's engine as it receded, getting back up into its place in the row of dinosaurs. That would occupy its driver a little while.

Breathing hard, shaken and hurting, I leaned back against the rock wall, facing the craggy barren expanse of the ravaged quarry. I might have been on the moon, only my moon buggy had crashed. But my nine millimeter had made the trip with me, still tucked in its hip holster. The ledge had decent width, maybe five feet, so that wasn't the issue. Getting back up top, a dozen feet above, was. And a secondary issue, no less crucial, was those three Chicago sports fans up there. One or two would be occupied with Susan, but one at least would be watching outside, like that fat nothing-but-neck guy had been when I came along.

So I headed along the ledge, away from the portable building, probably a hundred yards. I needed some distance from Susan's captors, but also I was looking for a rocky area I felt capable of climbing. I'd been in my share of situations, both in country and back home, but I had never been in one that required rock-climbing skills. Also, I was pushing fucking seventy.

The cold air, at least, seemed to help. It wasn't cold enough to be a problem—it just helped me stay alert. And when I found an area where the rocky wall looked friendly, I started my climb. I took my time. I wanted to rescue my daughter, like any good dad. But if they were holding her for ransom purposes, they'd keep her alive.

If killing me was the point, however, that had been accomplished, as far as they knew. They might be packing up to go, or maybe to drive down onto the quarry floor and make sure I hadn't miraculously crawled out of a pile of squashed metal. And in either case, part of "packing up" might be to dispose of Susan. On the other hand, if I got careless and fell to my death, I wouldn't be much help to anyone.

Just the same, I picked up the pace.

I found foot- and handholds and made good progress, with my aging knees threatening to kill me deader than the drop. I slipped once and my guts fell and hit hard down there, but the rest of me held on. Finally I got to the top and no one was waiting. But an opportunity was. Down where that bulldozer had shoved the Impala over the side, all three of Susan's captors were standing near the edge, staring into the pit.

Did that mean they'd already disposed of her?

Their voices carried.

"When's it gonna explode?" the fat-neck guy said.

"It ain't gonna fuckin' explode," the tall one said.

"It'll just burn," the oblong-faced guy said.

"When'll *that* start?" the fat-neck guy asked.

"I don't think ever," the tall one said.

Staying low, I headed into the darkness and cut behind that mound of gravel and the row of heavy machinery, too. I came around behind the portable building and looked in a window and she was in there, duct-taped to a metal-and-plastic chair, her mouth duct-taped too. She couldn't see me from this angle, but I could see her, and that was all that mattered. I was tempted to tap on the window, but that might alert the trio staring down at a car refusing to explode or burn.

I trotted around the portable building and planted myself with the nine mil in a two-handed, target-range stance, and yelled, *"Hey! Assholes!"*

It was self-indulgent, I know. But I had taken a hell of a fall and was half-covered in quarry dust, and the cold was starting to register, and muscles I didn't know I had were aching, with my knees really feeling for shit, and maybe I'd busted a rib. Or two. Calling out like that might have alerted them enough to pull or raise a weapon, right?

Wrong.

I fired off three rounds so fast, it was like one gunshot stuttering. It echoed across the quarry and each of those heads burst in bright bloody chunks and all three tumbled backward and disappeared. One landed with a metallic crunch, hitting what was left of the Impala.

That made me smile.

SIXTEEN

I stood at the edge of the precipice.

Looking in. Looking down.

The three men were dead all right, two splayed ass-up on the rocky floor like puppets with their strings snipped, if a string-snipped puppet could have a gaping ragged exit wound in the back of its wooden skull. The third, the oblong-headed Bulls fan, who'd bounced off the crushed car, had wound up on his back, agape with the split-second realization that a bullet was traveling through his brain.

I backed away and suddenly felt the winter chill. The situation, the activity, had…if not warmed me…numbed me. But now my breath was smoking like one of the distant chimneys of the clustered factory buildings at the far end of the quarry, across the road. They made products here out of all this limestone, but I was only vaguely aware of what those products were. The makings for cement, and steel and glass manufacturing. It was hard to know everything a quarry was capable of.

I looked off toward the road, that river road where it all began, and realized this lane came out not far from where, over four decades ago, I had killed three men, including the Broker, severing a tie that went back five years and most of my post-Vietnam civilian life. I didn't feel anything about it. I just noted it. The way you drive past a school you remember attending.

But that nickname—that moniker—the "code" designation (pompous prick, the Broker)—*Quarry*. Carved out of rock. Empty. Feeling nothing. But he'd been wrong, the Broker—if nothing else, I'd felt rage. I'd felt betrayal. And I'd acted on it.

Since then, for what it was worth, I'd been my own man, hadn't I? Not everyone's road. But mine.

You might be frowning, wondering why I didn't get the fuck over to that portable building and rescue my daughter. Well, a couple of things. She was already rescued. All I had to do was get her out of that chair she was duct-taped to. And you weren't a man approaching seventy who had been in a car that got shoved over a cliff and who had to climb the hell out and cling to a rocky ledge for life, then make his way to a position where he could climb up a dozen more feet of cliff before killing the three young men responsible.

Were you?

Nine mil in hand, I walked to the portable building, but did not go in. I checked every window. Susan was tied into that chair toward one end of the shabby structure, and a small enclosed office was at the other. I knocked on the window closest to her and, when she turned to it, smiled and gave her a thumbs up.

Her head went back, and even the strip of duct tape over her mouth couldn't hide her big obvious smile, and her body relaxed as if she'd been holding her breath for hours.

Looking in the various windows, I could see this was indeed a structure either out of use or in little use. The only furniture, beside the chair Susan was tied into, was a line of half a dozen metal folding chairs along a wall. The sole area of the rectangular structure I couldn't get a bead on, through the windows, was that office, where blinds were drawn.

Someone *could* be in there....

I went up the handful of steps and in through the door at Susan's end. As I entered, her head swiveled to me and tilted back, her eyes conveying more emotions than I can list. But when I raised a "hold it right there" palm, her eyes and forehead understandably frowned.

Before I did anything else, I needed to clear that fucking office.

The flimsy looking wall had a window at left with drawn blinds, a door in the middle, and at right an empty bulletin board, which was to my back when I reached for the knob, twisted it, and pushed through, staying low, fanning my nine mil around at...

...nothing.

Almost nothing. A beat-up metal desk with no chair—possibly missing the chair Susan had been tied up in—was the lone fixture. Those folding chairs out there and this desk may have been connected, in some fashion, with that row of heavy machinery. Workers getting assignments possibly.

Finally I returned the nine millimeter to the hip holster and went over to Susan and removed her duct-tape gag as carefully as I could.

She looked up at me, her gratitude compromised by her frustration. "So you thought you'd finally get around to me?"

"I had things to do."

She nodded and swallowed. "Those three...those shots I heard...?"

"Dead. They're on the quarry floor. We need to get out of here. Talk can wait. I don't think either of us wants to have to try explaining this to somebody."

But she wanted to talk anyway: "They got in the house somehow and grabbed me. Not long after you left to see Lehman. Held me till they got a phone call and then we rushed out."

I was behind her now, kneeling. I didn't have a knife or anything to cut the duct tape binding her. I started with her ankles, secured to the chair legs. The silver tape had been looped around enough times that it was tough to get a tear started, and then to keep it going. It took a while.

We talked some more as I worked at it.

I said, "Someone must've been watching from across River Drive."

"For what?"

"For me. This was about luring me here, at least in part. The idea, I think, was to get rid of the both of us....There. That's your ankles...."

"If they ruined my velvet jeans, I'll..."

"Kill them? Beat you to it." I was crouching, at work on her wrists. Again, the tape had been looped around and around, and not just her wrists themselves but the upper part of the chair legs. But I managed to get a tear started through the multiple layers.

The door at the far end opened.

I got slowly to my feet, with Susan's back next to me.

Jeffrey Kinman—in the same dark-blue blazer, light-blue shirt and darker-blue tie as earlier—stepped in and closed the door with his left hand. In his right hand was a revolver, which I recognized as a Colt Cobra .38—I had one myself.

At home.

But he didn't point it at us, and in fact he angled it to the floor wearing an expression that began as surprise before shifting into something like relief.

"Thank God," he said, sighing it. "My people called and said something suspicious was going on out here."

"Your people?" I asked.

He nodded. "I'm a part owner of the quarry—didn't you know? What the hell happened here? Are you two all right?"

I stepped out from behind Susan and said, "Is that how you're going to play it?"

"I don't follow."

And yet he hadn't made a move toward us, no rush to help me free the obviously captive Susan.

"Are you going to make me say," I said, "how ridiculous it is?"

"What is?"

"That you—not a security team—got sent to check this out?"

His laugh was barely audible. He raised the Cobra and smiled, and it was rather beautiful. Sam Cooke singing, "You Send Me." It occurred to me, in one of those odd extended moments you can experience in a tense situation, how much like Susan he was—a middle-aged man who looked much younger. Susan didn't look any older than mid-thirties. I hoped she lived to be my age and look like fifty.

"You need to ease that gun off your right hip," Kinman said, softly, smoothly, "with your left hand. Two fingers."

I did so, reaching over, extracting the weapon, then holding the grip by thumb and forefinger like a dead rat by the tail.

"Now toss it," he said, with just a little edge in his voice.

I shook my head. Not a threatening motion, just a slow, reasonable one. "If I toss this, and it hits hard, it could go off. I'm just going to set it down."

He thought about that. He didn't like it and his chin crinkled and his eyes tightened. But finally he nodded.

I made my aching knees lower me and I set the nine mil on the floor. Stood just as slowly.

"Now," Kinman said, "step away from it."

I stepped away from the nine mil and my daughter still taped to her chair. Cut the distance between myself and Kinman by a third or so, between him and her. Least I could do for her.

"Their car is out there," he said, with a nod toward the wall beyond which the Charger was still parked. "Where are *they*?"

I gave him a thumbs down.

His eyes widened, his head tilted back. "You killed them. All three of them."

I nodded. "They didn't suffer. Head shots. When they went over the edge and hit bottom, they didn't feel a thing."

He stared at me; his mouth yawned open. Then: "What kind of man are you, Quarry?"

"Ah. You *know* me."

His nods came slow. His smile showed just his upper teeth. "I know you. I recognized you today, at the Concort, but I knew you long before that. But I don't think you really know *me*, do you?"

"Sure I do. You're the Broker's son."

His head went back and his nostrils showed. He stayed that way for perhaps fifteen seconds, then asked, "How long have you known?"

"Suspected a while. Talked to an old reporter today who filled in a few blanks. Arnold Kinman married your mother because she was pregnant with you. It's exactly how the Broker would've handled a situation like that—paying your mother off with respectability, and Kinman with a bigger share of the business. With the bonus for himself of keeping his bed warm with both—one at a time, I suppose, although who knows? He was a kinky dude."

Kinman's jaw was trembling; his hand around the Cobra was, too. "You're a terrible man."

"Well, they say it takes one to know one. I wonder if this is what your mother would've wanted from her son? She was no saint—she did business with the Outfit, just as your father did... that is, your real father. But mostly she was just a smart, tough, hardworking woman, and a black woman at that, making her way to the top of a white man's world. You have to admire that. Too bad you take after your father."

His forehead tightened. "My father was a great man."

I laughed. "*Arnold Kinman* was a great man?"

"My *real* father! The man you call the Broker was the most successful, powerful man in this part of the world! Your lies don't change that."

I shook my head, slowly. "Such pride. But no feeling for Arnold Kinman? Didn't he make an honest woman out of your mama? Don't you have any room in your heart for him? A *little* gratitude maybe?"

The trembling was accelerating. "He was greedy and he was a pervert. I hated him and he hated me."

"Must hurt to have to carry his name."

His free hand became a fist and he shook it. "I will tell you something. I will reveal something to you."

"Please. By all means."

Now he smiled again and this time it was awful, nothing at all to do with what smiling was intended for. "I'm not sorry that hiring your death didn't work out. That the two I hired through Minneapolis didn't succeed, or my Chicago helpers, rest their stupid fuck-up souls. I will have to go to some lengths to clean up this mess, but it's well worth it. Killing you myself. Killing you *personally* will mean so very much, will warm winter nights like these. And you will die knowing that the lies you, and this awful woman, propagated about my father, in print, will…not…stand."

I let out a single laugh. "Oh, sure they will. I mean, what are you going to do, son? Go door to door buying up the copies? Every time you get a nice pile, have a little bonfire? Book burning never goes out of style. Of course, e-books don't burn for shit."

He swallowed. I'd shaken him. His eyes looked wet. "This… this quarry is where you killed him, isn't it?"

"Well, alongside the road near here, yes."

"That story about my father naming you for this place— that's true?"

"It is. Kind of poetic for a psychopath, don't you think?"

His chin tightened; forehead, too. "Do you *want* me to shoot you?"

"Of course not. I'm just trying to rattle you. You're one of those criminals who sits at desk and orders up violence like room service. You've never killed a man in your life, not really."

"Don't you begin to think I can't—"

I hit the deck as Susan rolled from her chair, her hands free now, free to scoop up the nine mil where I'd set it on the floor next to her. She even knew to click off the safety.

Kinman swung his Cobra her way but she fired first.

The bullet caught him in the throat and he stood there gurgling and weaving, his free hand going to his neck like a scarf too tight, and then her second shot traveled through his right eye and splashed the office window behind him forming a Christmas wreath of blood and brains.

He fell on his knees, though it was too late to pray, and flopped face forward, with the unfired Cobra still in hand.

I got to my feet and went to her. She handed me the nine mil as she stood there clawing off the remnants of her duct-tape bonds from her wrists.

"You okay?" I asked.

She nodded. "Sorry you had to stall so long. Bitch to get free."

Her face, so like her mother's, was as somber as if we were at a graveside service, not that either of us gave a shit about the dead fuck nearby. Well, I cared enough to see if he had any car keys in a pocket.

He did. A fob. I took her and we left him there. Neither of us had touched anything, so it was a quick exit, with me clicking off the fluorescent lights with an elbow. We went out into the cold, moon-swept night, where everything was still. Not still as death, though, because the whir and hum of the limestone quarry's factory remained, a distant soundtrack that you felt as much as heard.

We found Jeffrey Kinman's car—a metallic-bronze Corvette, recent model. He'd known how to live, the Broker's son, and of course he had died just fine. Knowing we'd have to wipe it clean and dump it somewhere when we got back to town made for a bittersweet ride.

For a while we didn't say anything.

We were going past downtown Davenport when she said, "Now you have something else on me."

"One killing."

"Don't forget the one in Minneapolis."

"Two killings. How many do you have on me?"

Her smile was barely there.

"Who's counting?" she said.

Daddy's little girl.

SEVENTEEN

By the time of the spring thaw, I felt fairly confident nothing was going to come back on me. I'd been here and there, spreading love everywhere I went, but apparently I hadn't left any DNA. Anyway, nobody showed up looking for me, from either side of the law.

Just the same, I had gone on a shopping spree at a gun show and now I had so much artillery stowed around the Sylvan Lake condo, the NRA would say, "Bro—let's not overdo!"

Susan visited me before the season kicked in, and on her first night here I took her to Ernie's On Gull Lake, the best year-round restaurant in Brainerd. She had an ahi tuna salad and I had the pan-fried walleye, and we were kind of awkward for a while. There'd been a few phone calls, but this was our first face time together without anybody trying to kill either or both of us, and we didn't know what to talk about. But over a slice of pistachio cake we shared, she brought up the book again.

"We should write it together," she said.

I shook my head.

"I'll be discreet," she said, leaning forward. "I'm not going to expose your secret identity or anything. I won't lead anybody to the Batcave."

I held up a hand. "Honey, I'll help you, answer your questions, and cheer you on. But I'm already writing my own book. And we're not competition. You're the non-fiction writer. I'm just churning out sleazy paperbacks."

"Which everybody assumes are fiction."

"Come on, kid. Could any of this really have happened? You can come up here and work on your book this summer—I have plenty of room, and you can bounce everything off me."

That's how we left it, though I agreed to come and spend some time at her place, too. Christmas and such. She gave me a big hug before she left and kissed me on the cheek.

Before she slipped out the door, she said, "Bye, Daddy," and I'll be honest. I teared up a little. But you know what a softy I am.

The very day Susan headed home, the phone rang.

"Hi," a voice said.

"Hi Luann."

It wasn't my first call from her. I'd given her my contact info—if there was any human on the planet besides my daughter I trusted, Luann was it—and she had kept me informed of whether anything we'd done on my Biloxi excursion had come back on her, or might still come back on me.

Nothing so far, and I doubted anything ever would.

"I was thinking about you, Johnny."

"I think about you, too, Luann."

"I was wondering."

"Yes?"

"Why don't you come visit me? With nothing to do. Biloxi isn't so bad. There must be worse places."

"I know. I try to drop by every forty years or so."

A long pause. Then:

"Why don't you come sooner than that, Johnny? Y'know, there's still eight 'Sweets' we haven't tried. I have a responsibility to make sure things maintain the high Fantasy Sweets standard. Cowboy looks fun. Honeymoon is traditional but a lot of guests love it."

"I'll book a flight."

On the plane, I found myself wondering if what was left of my future might be well spent with that abused girl who had grown into a strong woman. Luann was a tough, resilient, smart little cookie, and almost as rich as Janet had been.

I'd had one improbable happy ending in my life.

Who said I couldn't have another?

QUARRY'S HISTORY

I did not expect to be writing this novel.

The genesis was a conversation between Hard Case Crime editor/publisher Charles Ardai and myself about possible future Quarry novels. Charles thinks, rightly, that a long-running series needs something special in each new entry for the readers (and book buyers on the corporate side) to get excited about.

I said, "What about, *Quarry Meets the Bowery Boys*? Or *Son of Quarry*?"

I was kidding, of course, but Charles said, "I like that—*Son of Quarry*."

And I said, "Or maybe *Quarry's Daughter*."

I didn't have the heart to tell him that I would rather have written *Quarry Meets the Bowery Boys*.

A problem I had with the idea (the daughter one, as opposed to the one with Slip and Sach) was that it seemed logically to need to occur after *The Last Quarry* (2006), which I intended to be the last book chronologically in the series.

Well, honestly the last book about Quarry period.

Quarry's history is a convoluted one. He began at the University of Iowa Writers Workshop in 1971. He was based in part on a friend of mine who served multiple tours in Vietnam and who came home to a cheating wife—he was a funny, sweet guy who had learned to kill, which fascinated me. I had also long been interested in Audie Murphy, the most decorated combat soldier in the European Theater, who had gone on to be a movie star, with a private life that evidenced what we now call Post-Traumatic Stress Disorder.

And I felt Vietnam had changed America—it had numbed the nation by way of news coverage over TV dinners of body bags being loaded up, and kids being clubbed at the Democratic National Convention and shot on college campuses.

Finally, I was looking for a way to go beyond the anti-hero movies and novels typified by Richard Stark's Parker (and the film *Point Blank* in 1967). I had written *Bait Money* (1973), a virtual pastiche of Stark (a pseudonym of Donald E. Westlake), and indulged in the same safe manner of civilians never being killed and creating a distance between the anti-hero and the reader by way of third-person prose. Instead, I would write about a killer and in the first person. In the very first chapter, he would do something terrible, and if a reader couldn't take the heat, they could get out of Quarry's kitchen.

I was very proud of the concept—two concepts, really: the first-person protagonist as a hitman who initially had to solve the murder he committed, and that of the "list," which was my way of developing a series out of what had been conceived as a one-shot novel. The idea of a former hitman who hires out to the targets of current hitmen, to stop them and find out who hired them, still seems to me one of my best *noir* notions.

The original four Quarry novels were published by Berkley Books as paperback originals in 1976 and 1977. The first novel was written between 1971 and '73, and took a while to sell. When it did, and I was asked for three more novels about Quarry, I thought I might be developing my signature character —perhaps making my mark. Quarry struck me as unique, and frankly still does.

But I was not asked for further entries, and—considering those four books just another busted series—I went on about my business, returning to my Nolan series and starting the Nathan Heller historical saga. During that same period, however, I began getting fan letters about Quarry and, at Bouchercon and other mystery conventions, found myself approached by readers who were enthusiastic about my hitman. Quarry was clearly becoming a cult favorite.

I was chastened, however, by my mentor Don Westlake's dictum: "A cult success is seven readers short of the writer making a living."

Nonetheless, after the early success of *True Detective* (1983, the first Nathan Heller novel), I had the opportunity to write one more Quarry, which I did (*Primary Target*, 1987, republished by Hard Case Crime as *Quarry's Vote*). The publisher of that novel, responding to Quarry's cult success, also republished the first four novels with my preferred titles (Berkley had provided their own titles without bothering to run them past me—welcome to the world of the paperback-original author in the '70s). This was literally ten years after the initial four-book run.

Then Quarry went back to sleep, waking up only for an occasional short story. One of these, "A Matter of Principal" (1989), was much anthologized, and became a short film of the same name (2003) that I wrote and co-produced. Its success on the festival circuit led to a feature film version, *The Last Lullaby* (2008), which I co-wrote.

Around the time of the two films, I had been approached by Charles Ardai (who had collected the first two Nolan novels as *Two for the Money*) about the possibility of a new Quarry novel. My decision to say yes had in part to do with Charles promising to hire Robert McGinnis, the acclaimed artist of '50s and '60s paperback covers (and a James Bond movie poster artist), to do the cover.

But I also relished the opportunity to provide a definitive conclusion to the Quarry series. To write one more book....

Which I did, utilizing my initial, solo script for what became

The Last Lullaby. And, surprisingly (to me anyway), the book did rather well, getting some of the best reviews of my career, including a rare *Entertainment Weekly* notice. At some point Charles said, "It's too bad you wrote the last book in the series. It would be nice to do another."

And I said, "What about *The First Quarry*?"

Since signing on with Charles, I've done a total of ten additional Quarry novels and one graphic novel for Hard Case Crime. An HBO/Cinemax TV series has happened (*Quarry*, 2016), which led to the five early books being repackaged and reprinted by HCC. The TV show, for which I wrote a script, became a sort of origin story, taking Quarry back to his hitman days. Initially, I had written only about Quarry's last contract killing and segued into the "list" idea. Because of the TV show, I backtracked to a number of his jobs for the Broker, including *Quarry's Choice* (2015), introducing Luann in one of my two favorites in the series (the other is *The Wrong Quarry*, 2014, a "list" novel).

I have attempted, as best a math-challenged person like myself is capable, of maintaining Quarry's continuity while jumping around chronologically. I am sure there are goofs. I am not perfect, and Quarry is not necessarily a reliable narrator.

My reluctance to do a book following *The Last Quarry*, which was after all meant to be the last Quarry, was mirrored by Charles wanting a new Nolan novel, a series I had ended with *Spree* (1987). But then I got a notion for a sort of coda for Nolan, which became *Skim Deep* (2020) and spurred the idea to do the same for Quarry. For various reasons, the daughter needed to show up after *The Last Quarry*, and a coda made that possible, without disrupting my perverse desire to give my hero (and I consider him a hero, not an anti-hero) a happy ending.

Is this second "last" Quarry novel the last Quarry novel? We'll see....

Which leads me to needing to thank a few people, and Charles Ardai is at the top of that list. He cajoles, he reasons, he drives one crazy, but in a good way. Thank you, Charles.

My wife, Barb—with whom I write the cozy *Antiques* mysteries—was as usual both a helpful editor and a great sounding board. Her story sense is stellar and her ability—when I am considering options for a scene or even a chapter—to guide me in the best direction is uncanny.

Thanks also to my frequent collaborator, Matthew V. Clemens and our "forensics" guy, Chris Kauffman, who aided us on the CSI novels. And my usual, but no less sincere, thanks to my friend and agent, Dominick Abel.

One last note. You need not point out to me that one of Quarry's aliases, Keller, is the name of Lawrence Block's hitman character. This is neither homage nor theft. The first Keller novel came out after its first use in my story "Guest Services," although Larry's hitman appeared in a short story before that in *Playboy*. Unfortunately I did not always read *Playboy* for the articles, or the stories, and was unaware of this. I used the name here for consistency's sake.

In my defense, I know Larry was aware of Quarry because he read the first book on its initial publication, loaned to him by Don Westlake, who passed along Larry's comments to me. And, for that matter, his Keller once came to my hometown, Muscatine, Iowa, to fulfill a contract. I think he may have knocked on my door....

Max Allan Collins
February 2021

WANT MORE QUARRY?

Try These Other Quarry Novels From
MAX ALLAN COLLINS *and*
HARD CASE CRIME...

The First Quarry

The ruthless hitman's first assignment: kill a philandering professor who has run afoul of some very dangerous men.

Quarry in the Middle

When two rival casino owners covet the same territory, guess who gets caught in the crossfire...

The Last Quarry

Retired killer Quarry gets talked into one last contract—but why would anyone want a beautiful librarian dead...?

Quarry's Ex

An easy job: protect the director of a low-budget movie. Until the director's wife turns out to be a woman out of Quarry's past.

The Wrong Quarry

Quarry zeroes in on the grieving family of a missing cheerleader. Does the hitman's hitman have the wrong quarry in his sights?

Or Read On for a Sample Chapter From
The Book Where We First Meet Luann,
QUARRY'S CHOICE!

ONE

I had been killing people for money for over a year now, and it had been going fine. You have these occasional unexpected things crop up, but that's life.

Really, to be more exact about it, I'd been killing people for *good* money for over a year. Before that, in the Nam soup, I had been killing people for chump change, but then the Broker came along and showed me how to turn the skills Uncle Sugar had honed in me into a decent living.

I'll get to the Broker shortly, but you have to understand something: if you are a sick fuck who wants to read a book about some lunatic who gets off on murder, you are in the wrong place. I take no joy in killing. Pride, yes, but not to a degree that's obnoxious or anything.

As the Broker explained to me from right out of the gate, the people I'd be killing were essentially already dead: somebody had decided somebody else needed to die, and was going to have it done, which was where I came in. *After* the decision had been made. I'm not guilty of murder any more than my Browning nine millimeter is.

Guns don't kill people, some smart idiot said, *people kill people*—or in my case, people have some other person kill people.

There's a step here I've skipped and I better get to it. When I came home from overseas, I found my wife in bed with a guy. I didn't kill him, which I thought showed a certain restraint on my part, and when I went to talk to him about our "situation" the next day, I hadn't gone there to kill him, either. If I had, I'd have brought a fucking gun.

But he was working under this fancy little sports car, which like my wife had a body way too nice for this prick, and when he saw me, he looked up at me all sneery and said, "I got nothing to say to you, bunghole." And I took umbrage. Kicked the fucking jack out.

Ever hear the joke about the ice cream parlor? The cutie behind the counter asks, *"Crushed nuts, sir?"* *"No,"* the customer replies, *"rheumatism."* Well, in my wife's boyfriend's case it was crushed nuts.

They didn't prosecute me. They were going to at first, but then there was some support for me in the papers, and when the DA asked me if I might have *accidently* jostled the jack, I said, "Sure, why not?" I had enough medals to make it messy in an election year. So I walked.

This was on the west coast, but I came from the Midwest, where I was no longer welcome. My father's second wife did not want a murderer around—whether she was talking about the multiple yellow ones or the single-o white guy never came up. My father's first wife, my mother, had no opinion, being dead.

The Broker found me in a shit pad in L.A. on a rare bender —I'm not by nature a booze hound, nor a smoker, not even a damn coffee drinker—and recruited me. I would come to find out he recruited a lot of ex-military for his network of contract killers. Vietnam had left a lot of guys fucked-up and confused and full of rage, not necessarily in that order, and he could sort of…channel it.

The contracts came from what I guess you'd call underworld sources. Some kills were clearly mob-related; others were civilians who were probably dirty enough to make contacts with the kind of organized crime types who did business with the Broker—a referral kind of deal. Thing was, a guy like me never knew who had taken the contract. That was the reason for a Broker—he was our agent and the client's buffer.

Right now, maybe eighteen months since he'd tapped me on the shoulder, the Broker was sitting next to me in a red-button-tufted booth at the rear of an underpopulated restaurant and lounge on a Tuesday evening.

He was wearing that white hair a little longer now, sprayed in place, with some sideburns, and the mustache was plumper now, wider too, but nicely trimmed. I never knew where that deep tan came from—Florida vacations? A tanning salon? Surely not the very cold winter that Davenport, Iowa, had just gone through, and that's where we were—at the hotel the Broker owned a piece of, the Concort Inn near the government bridge over the Mississippi River, connecting Davenport and Rock Island, Illinois.

Specifically, we were in the Gay '90s Lounge, one of the better restaurants in the Iowa/Illinois Quad Cities, a study in San Francisco-whorehouse red and black. The place seemed to cater to two crowds—well-off diners in the restaurant area and a singles-scene "meat market" in the bar area. A small combo—piano, bass and guitar—was playing jazzy lounge music, very quietly. A couple couples were upright and groping on the postage-stamp dance floor, while maybe four tables were dining, money men with trophy wives. Or were those mistresses?

The Broker sat with his back to the wall and I was on the curve of the booth next to him. Not right next to him. We weren't cozy or anything. Often he had a bodyguard with him, another of his ex-military recruits—the Rock Island Arsenal was just across the government bridge and that may have been a source.

But tonight it was just the two of us, a real father-and-son duo. We'd both had the surf and turf (surf being shrimp, not lobster—my host didn't throw his dough around) and the Broker was sipping coffee. I had a Coke—actually, I was on my second. One of my few vices.

The Broker was in a double-knit navy two-button blazer with wide lapels, a wide light-blue tie and a very light-blue shirt, collars in. His trousers were canary yellow, but fortunately you couldn't see that with him sitting. A big man, six two with a slender but solid build, with the handsome features of a sophisticated guy in a high-end booze ad in *Playboy*. Eyes light gray. Face grooved for smile and frown lines but otherwise smooth. Mid-forties, though with the bearing of an even older man.

I was in a tan leisure suit with a light brown shirt. Five ten, one-hundred and sixty pounds, brown hair worn a little on the long side but not enough to get heckled by a truck driver. Sideburns but nothing radical. Just the guy sitting next to you on the bus or plane who you forgot about the instant you got where you were going. Average, but not so average that I couldn't get laid now and then.

"How do you like working with Boyd?" he asked. He had a mellow baritone and a liquid manner.

I had recently done a job with Boyd. Before that was a solo job and then five with a guy named Turner who I wound up bitching about to Broker.

Contracts were carried out by teams, in most cases, two-man ones—a passive and an active member. The passive guy went in ahead of time, sometimes as much as a month but at the very least two weeks, to get the pattern down, taking notes and running the whole surveillance gambit. The active guy came in a week or even less before the actual hit, utilizing the passive player's intel. Sometimes the passive half split town shortly after the active guy showed; sometimes the surveillance guy hung around if the getaway was tricky or backup might be needed.

"Well," I said, "you *do* know he's a fag."

The Broker's white eyebrows rose. It was like two caterpillars getting up on their hind legs. "No! Tough little fella like that? That hardly seems credible. Could you have misread the signs? You must be wrong, Quarry."

That wasn't my name. My name is none of your business. Quarry is the alias or code moniker that the Broker hung on me. All of us working for him on active/passive teams went by single names. Like Charo or Liberace.

"Look, Broker," I said, after a sip of Coke from a tall cocktail glass, "I don't give a shit."

"Pardon?"

"I said I don't care who Boyd fucks as long as doesn't fuck up the job."

Surprise twinkled in the gray eyes and one corner of his mouth turned up slightly. "Well, that's a very broad-minded attitude, Quarry."

"A broad-minded attitude is exactly what Boyd doesn't have."

The Broker frowned at me. He had the sense of humor of a tuna. "If you wish, Quarry, I can team you with another of my boys—"

I stopped that with a raised hand. "I think Boyd is ideal for my purposes. He prefers passive and I prefer active. You're well aware that sitting stakeout bores the shit out of me, whereas Boyd has a streak of voyeur in him."

"Well, that's hardly enough to recommend him as your permanent partner."

"I'm not marrying him, Broker. Just working with him. And anyway, I like his style—he's a regular guy, a beer-drinking, ball-team-following Joe. Fits in, blends in, does not the fuck stand out."

Understand, Boyd was no queen—he was on the small side

but sturdy, with a flat scarred face that had seen its share of brawls; his hair was curly and thick and brown, with bushy eyebrows and mustache, like so many were wearing. Also he had the kind of hard black eyes you see on a shark. Good eyes for this business.

With a what-the-hell wave, I said, "Let's go with Boyd."

Broker smiled, lifting his coffee cup. "Boyd it shall be."

You probably noticed that the Broker talked like a guy who'd read Shakespeare when to the rest of us English literature meant Ian Fleming.

"So," I said, "four jobs last year, and the one last month. That par for the course?"

He nodded. "Your advance should be paid in full by the end of this year. With that off the books, you'll have a very tidy income for a relative handful of jobs per annum."

"Jobs that carry with them a high degree of risk."

"Nothing in life is free, Quarry."

"Hey, I didn't just fall off a turnip truck."

A smile twitched below the mustache. "So, they have *turnip* trucks in Ohio, do they?"

"I wouldn't know. I've never been on a farm in my life. Strictly a townie." I leaned in. "Listen, Broker, I appreciate the free meal...keeping in mind nothing is free, like you said...but if you have no objection, I'm going to head home now."

He gestured like a *Price Is Right* model to a curtain opening onto a grand prize. "You're welcome to stay another night, my young friend. Several nights, if you like. You've earned a rest and a...bonus, perhaps? Possibly by way of a working girl? Something young and clean? Check out the redhead and the brunette, there at the end of the bar...."

"No thanks, Broker." He seemed unusually generous tonight. "I just want to head back."

"But it's eight o'clock, and so many miles before you sleep."

I shrugged. "I like to drive at night. Why, is there something else you want to go over?"

It had felt throughout the meal that something more was hanging in the air than the question of Boyd as my official passive partner.

He lowered his head while raising his eyes to me. There was something careful, even cautious about it. Very quietly, though no one was seated anywhere near us, he asked, "How do you feel about a contract involving...a woman?"

With a shrug, I said, "I don't care who hires me. Hell, I don't even *know* who hires me, thanks to you."

"Not what I mean, Quarry."

I grinned at him. "Yeah, I knew that. Just rattling your chain, Broker."

He sighed, weight-of-the-world. "You know, I really should resent your insolence. Your impertinence. Your insubordination."

"Is that all? Can't you think of anything else that starts with an 'I'?"

That made him smile. Maybe a little sense of humor at that. "Such a rascal."

"Not to mention scamp."

Now he raised his head and lowered his eyes to me. Still very quiet, as if hunting wabbits. "I mean, if the...person you were dispatched to dislodge were of the female persuasion. Would that trouble you?"

That was arch even for the Broker.

I said, "I don't think it's possible to persuade anybody to be a female. Maybe you should check with Boyd on that one."

"Quarry...a straight answer please."

"You won't get one of those out of Boyd."

He frowned, very disapproving now.

I pawed the air. "Okay, okay. No clowning. No, I have no

problem with 'dislodging' the fairer sex. It's been my experience that women are human beings, and human beings are miserable creatures, so what the heck. Sure."

He nodded like a priest who'd just heard a confessor agree to a dozen Hail Mary's. "Good to know. Good to know. Now, Quarry, there may be upon occasion jobs in the offing…so to speak…that might require a willingness to perform as you've indicated."

Jesus. I couldn't navigate that sentence with a fucking sextant. So I just nodded.

"May I say that I admire your technique. I don't wish to embarrass you, Quarry, but you have a certain almost surgical skill…"

That's what they said about Jack the Ripper.

"…minimizing discomfort for our…subjects."

"Stop," I said. "I'll blush."

He leaned back in the booth. "Not everyone came back from their terrible overseas ordeal as well-adjusted as you, Quarry. Some of my boys have real problems."

"Imagine that. I'd like some dessert, if that's okay."

I'd spotted a waiter with a dessert tray.

The Broker gave a little bow and did that Arab hand roll thing like he was approaching a pasha. Jesus, this guy. "It would be my pleasure, Quarry. There is a quite delicious little hotfudge sundae we make here, with local ice cream. Courtesy of the Lagomarcino family."

"Didn't I do one of them in Chicago last September?"

"Uh, no. Different family. Similar name."

"Rose by any other."

Knowing I planned to book it after the meal, I had already stowed my little suitcase in the backseat of my Green Opel GT out in the parking lot.

So in fifteen minutes more or less, the Broker—after signing for the meal—walked me out into a cool spring night, the full moon casting a nice ivory glow on the nearby Mississippi, its surface of gentle ripples making the kind of interesting texture you find on an alligator.

The Concort Inn was a ten-story slab of glass and steel, angled to provide a better river view for the lucky guests on that side. The hotel resided on about half a city block's worth of cement, surrounded by parking. The lights of cars on the nearby government bridge, an ancient structure dating back to when nobody skimped on steel, were not enough to fend off the gloom of the nearby seedy warehouse area that made a less than scenic vista for the unlucky guests on the hotel's far side. The hotel's sign didn't do much to help matters, either, just a rooftop billboard with some under-lighting. Four lanes of traffic cutting under the bridge separated the parking lot from the riverfront, but on a Tuesday night at a quarter till nine, "traffic" was an overstatement.

We paused outside the double doors we'd just exited. No doorman was on duty. Which was to say, no doorman was ever on duty: this was Iowa. The Broker was lighting up a cheroot, and for the first time I realized what he most reminded me of: an old riverboat gambler. It took standing here on the Mississippi riverfront to finally get that across to me. All he needed one of those Rhett Butler hats and Bret Maverick string ties. And he should probably lose the yellow pants.

"Broker," I said, "you *knew* Boyd was gay."

"Did I?" He smiled a little, his eyebrows rising just a touch, his face turned a flickery orange by the kitchen match he was applying to the tip of the slender cigar.

"Of course you did," I said. "You research *all* of us down to how many fillings we have, what our fathers did for a living, and what church we stopped going to."

He waved the match out. "Why would I pretend not to have

known that Boyd is a practicing homosexual? Perhaps it's just something I missed."

"Christ, Broker, he lives in Albany with a hairdresser. And I doubt at this point he needs any practice."

He gave me a grandiloquent shrug. "Perhaps I thought you might have been offended had I mentioned the fact."

"I told you. He can sleep with sheep if he wants. Boy sheep, girl sheep, I don't give a fuck. But why hold that back?"

He let out some cheroot smoke. He seemed vaguely embarrassed. "One of my boys strongly objected to Boyd. But somehow my instincts told me that you would not. That you would be—"

"Broad-minded."

"I was going to say forward-thinking." He folded his arms and gave me a professorly look. "It's important we not be judgmental individuals, Quarry. That we be open-minded, unprejudiced, so that our professionalism will hold sway."

"Right the fuck on," I said.

He frowned at that, crudity never pleasing him, and the big two-tone green Fleetwood swung into the lot from the four-lane with the suddenness and speed of a boat that had gone terribly off course. The Caddy slowed as it cut across our path, the window on the rider's side down. The face looking out at us was almost demonic but that was because its Brillo-haired owner was grimacing as he leaned the big automatic against the rolled-down window and aimed it at us, like a turret gun on a ship's deck. A .45, I'd bet.

But I had taken the Broker down to the pavement, even before the thunder of it shook the night and my nine millimeter was out from under my left arm and I was shooting back at the bastard just as a second shot rocketed past me, eating some metal and glass, close enough for me to feel the wind of it but not touching me, and I put two holes in that grimace, both in the forehead, above either eye, and blood was

welling down over his eyes like scarlet tears as the big vehicle
tore out.

The last thing I saw was his expression, the expression of a
screaming man, but he wasn't screaming, because he was dead.
And dead men not only don't tell tales, they don't make *any*
fucking sound, including screams.

I didn't chase them. Killing the shooter was enough. Maybe
too much.

The Broker, looking alarmed, said something goddamned
goofy to me, as I was hauling him up. "You wore a gun to *dinner*
with me? Are you insane, man? This is neutral territory."

"Tell those assholes," I said, "and by the way—you're welcome."

He was unsteady on his feet.

The desk manager came rushing out and the Broker glanced
back and shouted, "Nothing to see here! Children with cherry
bombs. Franklin, keep everybody inside."

Franklin, an efficient little guy in a vest and bow tie (more
riverboat shit), rounded up the curious, handing out drink chits.

There was a stone bench near the double doors and I sat
Broker down on it and plopped beside him.

"You okay?" I asked.

He looked blister pale. "My dignity is bruised."

"Well, it doesn't show in those pants. I killed the shooter."

"Good. That should send a message."

"Yeah, but who to? And if you correct me with 'to whom,' I'll
shoot you myself."

He frowned at me, more confusion than displeasure. "Did
you get the license?"

"Not the number. Mississippi plates, though."

That seemed to pale him further. "Oh dear."

Oh dear, huh? Must be bad.

"Somebody may call the cops," I said. "Not everybody who

heard that, and maybe saw it, is in having free drinks right now."

He nodded. "You need to leave. Now."

"No argument." I had already put the gun away. They weren't coming back, not with a guy shot twice in the face they weren't. Anyway, by now "they" was one guy, driving a big buggy into a night that was just getting darker.

I patted him on the shoulder. That was about as friendly as we'd ever got. "Sure you're okay?"

"I'm fine. I'll handle this. Go."

I went, and the night I was driving into was getting darker, too. But I had the nine millimeter on the rider's seat to keep me company....